The Butterfly Mafia

By: Fumiya Payne

Lock Down Publications
P.O. Box 944
Stockbridge, GA 30281
www.lockdownpublications.com

Like our page on Facebook: Lock Down Publications
www.facebook.com/lockdownpublications.ldp

Stay Connected with Us!

Text LOCKDOWN to 22828 to stay up-to-date with new releases, sneak peaks, contests and more…
Or CLICK HERE to sign up.

Like our page on Facebook:
Lock Down Publications: Facebook

Join Lock Down Publications/The New Era Reading Group

Visit our website:
www.lockdownpublications.com

Follow us on Instagram:
Lock Down Publications: Instagram

Email Us: We want to hear from you!

Acknowledgments...

As always, all praises to the Most High. You and I know what's going on, so I'll keep it short. But remember when I would spend hours trying to express my deepest gratitude? Forgetful of the fact that you read hearts. Silly me!

Ca$h... I can't speak for no other woman or man, but I can personally and truthfully say that since I've known you, your feet have been firmly planted on morals and principles.

Shawn... I'll forever remember your feedback to my very first novel. I was a literary newborn on unsteady legs, and your encouragement was the nourishment I so desperately needed. So from the very bottom of my heart, thank you, Queen.

To my readers... the name Fumiya is a symbolization of suffering. So as the direct offspring of Payne & Suffering, my primary purpose is to give strength and support to those who've been forced to foot their journey's under similar conditions. And though my struggle continues, I tearfully pray I'll pen something in my poetry or stories that will assist someone else in their advancement through adversity.

May the pure hearted prevail,
Fumiya Payne.

Chapter 1

"Ooh, this shit feel so good, baby!" a dark-skinned woman wailed while riding a man backwards in the backseat of an SUV. With her skirt hiked up around her waist, she was alternating her movements between a rhythmic bounce and a circular grind.

Gripping a Glock in one hand and a soft cheek in the other, the man, Pee-Wee, was amazed at the amount of cream her yoni was leaking over his condom-covered penis.

"I'ma miss you so much!" the woman continued, as she ground into his pelvis with a pleasurable grimace.

When Pee-Wee announced in a hurried tone that he was on the verge of coming, she quickly rose up, turned to snatch off the condom and further amazed him with a magic trick he'd known only few to perform.

"Ohhh, shit!" Pee-Wee groaned, as she sucked his entire shaft down the neck of her oral vacuum.

After swallowing every salty spurt of his syrupy semen, she lovingly licked around the head while gently massaging his balls.

"You gon' make sure ain't nothing left in them bitches, huh?" he smiled down at her.

"You better know it," she smiled back. "Another bitch jaws will lock up before she get some more nut up out of him. This my dick."

Once they had fixed their clothing, Pee-Wee concealed the weapon at the small of his back and the smiling couple exited the SUV.

Packed with a multitude of people and a variety of vehicles, the energy at Belle Isle could be summarized as lively. A popular park in Detroit that was surrounded by a large island, it was a gathering site that summoned the likes of all types. And on this particularly sunny Sunday afternoon, there wasn't a shortage of scheming savages, boastful brick boys, or fashionable females who flourished from the art of finesse.

"Babe, you sure you can't come through later and spend the night with me?" the woman pouted, placing her arms around Pee-Wee's neck.

He shook his head, "Nah, I already told you I gotta kick it with my peoples. So respect what I'm saying."

"Yeah, alright," she conceded in disappointment. "But you better make sure you call me as soon as you can. And I'ma miss you, and I love you. And whatever you need me to do, consider it done."

As she strutted off, Pee-Wee stared after the enticing jiggle of her plump cheeks before turning to address his brother, who had stood guard outside the truck during his backseat affair. "Bro, if she give that box away while I'm gone, I want you to give her a vasectomy with your bare hands."

Otha's mouth curled into a slight grin, as he envisioned himself performing what he knew would be a painful procedure.

Originally from Flint, Michigan, Pee-Wee and Otha had migrated to the 'Motor' several years ago, per the request of their female cousins, Mecca and Unique. After witnessing the women orchestrate the most revengeful, but rewarding exploit they'd known of thus far, they began to faithfully follow behind them as if they were female Messiahs. And unbeknownst to the crowd of people among whom they were presently gathered, Pee-Wee and Otha were responsible for some of the city's most monstrous murders and daring robberies.

"Damn, O, what up?" Pee-Wee yelled over the blaring music that came from a nearby car. "Nigga, it's a thousand bitches out here. You mean to tell me you don't see nothing you like?" When he didn't respond, Pee-Wee leaned over to playfully bump into him. "Come on, bro, you gon' be alright. It's only for six months."

As a result of not controlling his anger, a verbal dispute had led to Pee-Wee breaking a man's nose in a public setting. Although the victim had been persuaded to discontinue his court appearances, the incident was on camera, which allowed the prosecutor to proceed without his presence or testimony. So to avoid a trial that would be impossible to win, Pee-Wee pled out to a lesser charge and was sentenced to six months in county.

"That's easy for you to say," Otha replied without making eye contact. "Because you'll be confined to a kennel, where your biggest responsibility is keeping your bed made."

"And while I'm in there making that bitch military-style," Pee-Wee smiled. "You gon' be out here holding it down. You gon' bring your crazy ass to see me every week, and I'ma need you to sneak me a phone up in there, too."

Otha turned to him, "How the fuck you expect me to do that?"

"Shit, nigga, you gotta stick that mu'fucka up in your ass. Just make sure you wrap it up good."

Once they stopped laughing, Pee-Wee checked the time on his gold A.P. watch. "Man, where the fuck is Mecca and them at? They was supposed to be here like a half-hour ago."

Otha scoffed, "As if you don't know, they'll be late for their own funerals."

Just then, the atmosphere was pervaded by the loud roar of a three-wheeled Harley Davidson as it entered the park.

Ridden by two helmeted people in leather racing suits, the customized "Freewheeler" had bobtail fenders, slash cut chrome pipes, and a powerful V-Twin engine. Painted all-white with royal-blue accents, the bike was a beauty to behold. Drawing complimentary comments and salivating stares, the Freewheeler cruised through the crowded lot in search of a place to park.

"I know these bitches ain't came through on no Harley," Pee-Wee laughed, as it headed towards them. "They doing the most now."

Otha frowned, wondering when the women had learned how to ride a bike. As he was on the verge of voicing his suspicion to Pee-Wee, the rider on back removed a short-barreled machine gun from inside its jacket and aimed it in their direction.

Before either man could reach or run, the gunman opened fire in a sweeping motion, distributing the lead in equal portions.

Amid the chaotic sounds of screeching tires and fearful screams, the gunman hopped off the Harley and hurried toward Pee-Wee and Otha, who were both on the ground, wide-eyed and wheezing.

Of all the places in which they had predicted their deaths would occur, neither brother thought to include a public park... in broad daylight.

The gunman paused over Pee-Wee, lifted its leg high into the air and used the bottom of a steel-toed boot to crush his skull with several vicious stomps.

Having managed to lay hold of his weapon, Otha was weakly raising it, when the gunman punted the pistol clear across the parking lot, breaking several of his fingers in the process.

Upon removing a picture from inside its jacket, the gunman bent to bring it before Otha's face. The instant his eyes registered recognition, the gunman stepped on his neck to keep his head in place, then fired enough rounds to turn his dome into a stadium.

8

Replacing the photo inside the jacket, but tossing the murder weapon in the water, the gunman jogged back to bike and climbed on.

As the driver revved the engine before taking off in a loud rumble, neither rider paid attention to a purple coupe that sped into the park.

On the mid level of a parking garage, a beautiful blonde named Lo-Lo was seated behind the wheel of a Tahoe. With alluring blue eyes and a diamond stud in her left nostril, she was casually clothed in a form-fitting tracksuit. Constantly checking the time, Lo-Lo was nervously tapping one of her pointed nails on the center console, when she heard the rumbling sound of an approaching motorcycle. Sighing in relief, she pressed a button to mechanically raise the rear hatch and exited the truck.

As Lo-Lo was standing at the trunk, withdrawing clothes from a shopping bag, the Harley pulled around to the driver side of the Tahoe and parked. Quickly dismounting the stolen bike, the riders removed their helmets to surprisingly reveal the faces of two light skinned females, who both had a blue butterfly tattooed beneath the corner of their left eye.

As they were stripping off their racing gear and gloves, Lo-Lo was stuffing the items inside a heavy-duty trash bag. Her job was to destroy all physical evidence related to the double murder.

Once they had changed into regular clothing, there was a noticeable difference in the appearance of the two females.

Her birth name, Asha, the driver of the Harley had doll-like features, a shapely figure, and dark-colored hair that was presently in a topknot. Standing at 5'6", she was wearing gray leggings and a Polo sweater that clung to her generous chest.

Bearing a slight resemblance to the female rapper, Young M.A., the shooter had on a red pair of Vapor Maxes, a Jordan hoodie, and designer jeans that hung several inches below the band of her briefs. Aside from having braided hair and a mouthful of sparkling diamonds, Noni's masculine mannerisms made it clear that she was a bonafide stud. But in spite of their differences, the two women shared a bond that exceeded their sexuality; for Asha and Noni were twin sisters.

As Lo-Lo and Asha climbed inside the Tahoe, Noni grabbed an AR-556 assault rifle from the trunk area. Modified to a fully automatic, the 'Blackout' was impregnated with a hundred-round drum.

"Really?" Asha asked, looking over her shoulder as Noni slid in the backseat with the large weapon.

"I ain't going back in that cage, Twin," Noni soberly stated, racking a round into the gun's chamber. "So if y'all see cherries and berries... I advise you to duck."

***

Back at Belle Isle, the occupants of the purple coupe were standing outside the car. While en route to the park, they'd took in the frantic dispersal of cars and instinctively sensed that whatever had happened involved their own. And their suspicions were confirmed when they came upon their two favorite cousins, who were lifelessly lying in pools of blood.

"We should've been here," Unique regretfully mumbled, feeling the bitter sting of guilt behind their late arrival.

"Maybe not," Mecca replied, as she reached down to lower the lids of Otha's eyes. "Because maybe then it would've been four dead bodies. So see our delay as a blessing, instead of a burden."

Without a witness in sight and the sounds of sirens rising by the second, the women knew it was pointless to hang around. So, after assuring Pee-Wee and Otha that their deaths would be avenged, the sisters slid back in the coupe and drove off.

"We've gained too much to give it all back," Mecca said as Unique steered them through the city's east side. "And this could or could not be connected to our past. But either way, we definitely gotta figure out who did this." Unique nodded in agreement.

"Facts." Mecca turned her piercing green eyes toward Unique and coldly inserted, "And the same way we did in the past... we gon' have to force whoever did this to salute our muthafucking savagery!"

The elder sister of Unique by fourteen months, Mecca had a cunning mind that was belied by beautiful features. The strength and extent of her savagery had been established after the death of their younger sibling, Amiri. Because not only had Mecca sought and attained revenge on all parties involved in her murder, but she had used the illusion of love to relieve them of their life savings. Needless to say, Mecca was not the woman with whom you wanted to wage a war. But neither were the twins.

Chapter 2

"...Middle finger to my daddy/ Why a sucka had to fuck my mammy?/ Left us, and he traumatized us badly/ Created him a savage/ Hustle hard just to get cabbage/ 'Cause growing up, a bitch never had it/ What you know about struggle?"

A City Girls song was crooning through the speakers of the Tahoe as Lo-Lo left-handedly steered it through the city's gritty streets. Beside her, Asha was gazing out the passenger window in deep thought. And Noni was slouched in the backseat, with the assault rifle dutifully draped over the denim of her jeans.

Upon entering a suburban section on the north side of town, Lo-Lo circled the block before pulling into the driveway of a two-story house. Lowering the music, Lo-Lo laid a comforting hand on Asha's forearm.

"What's up, Asha? You butter, girl?"

"Yeah, I'm smooth," she nodded, then leaned over to hug one of her most trusted and loyal friends.

"B.F.M.!" Lo-Lo hissed into her ear with conviction.

"For life!" Asha replied with equaled emphasis.

When the two women disengaged, Noni extended her arm up front to shake hands with Lo-Lo. "Stay alert, love." With Noni shouldering the rifle, her and Asha attentively exited the truck.

Lo-Lo waited until they were safely inside before backing out. Normally, she'd join them. But after today's events, she respected the privacy needed among the two siblings. So, she reluctantly drove off, hoping closure would manage to quiet the anguishing wail within their troubled souls.

Back at the condo, the sisters wordlessly walked upstairs and paused at its top landing. Removing the rifle from Noni's hand, Asha laid it aside and pulled her twin into a motherly embrace. The eldest by ninety-six seconds, she's played the protector's role since they were toddlers.

"They gone, love," Asha whispered while rubbing a soothing hand over Noni's head. "So, we can start to live now."

Inside her personal bathroom, Asha placed a black Beretta on the basin before adjusting the shower's temperature to a near scalding degree. It was as if she was expecting to burn away the pain of her past. Untying her shoulder-length hair, Asha disrobed to reveal a large tattoo that covered majority of her back. Colored aqua, blue, and black, it was the drawing of a deeply-detailed butterfly with blood trickling from its sharpened fangs. And in Old English lettering, the insect was encased within the words: Butterfly Mafia.

With her head down as she stood under the water, Asha raised a hand to her face and slowly traced it over a scar that was beneath the blue butterfly. A scar that resulted from a life-alternating night that had not only forced her and Noni to prematurely enter adulthood, but one that also warranted the occurrence of today's events

Flashback

Sixteen-year-olds, Asha and Lo-Lo were standing in the girl's bathroom, checking their hair and makeup. Two of the most popular girls in school, it was imperative they maintain a faultless appearance.

Meanwhile, a solemn-faced Noni was posted near the door, with her arms defensively crossed and the sole of a Nike planted on the wall.

"Girl, guess who tried to step to me," Lo-Lo said in between applying a coat of lip gloss.

"Who?"

"Chubba, girl."

"You talking about that fat nigga from Whittier?"

"Yeah, girl. And I told his slow ass I don't know what the fuck he expect me to pour from an empty cup."

"Did he know what you meant?"

"Most definitely didn't!"

In midst of their laughter, a Latino girl rushed into the bathroom."

They about to jump your brother," she breathlessly informed Lo-Lo.

Racing from the restroom, they found her brother, Lance, in the hallway surrounded by several seniors.

"What the fuck is all this, Doony?" Lo-Lo demanded, addressing one of the three boys with whom she was most familiar.

"I caught his lil thieving ass trying to break in my locker."

Lo-Lo shot a brother a questioning glance, to which he shrugged, "I ain't know it was his, sis."

Two years younger than Lo-Lo, Lance had a scrawny build, a loner's demeanor, and sad brown eyes that didn't align. But outside of that, the boy had a heart of gold.

"So how you want to handle this?" Lo-Lo said, redirecting her attention to Doony. "Because clearly this my little brother. And like you said, you caught him. Which means nothing was taken. So let's just see this for the mistake it was and move on."

For the sake of onlookers, Doony pridefully replied, "To make sure it don't happen again, I think this nigga need to be taught a lesson. 'Cause if he old enough to be stealing, then he old enough to get that ass whooped. And I don't give a fuck about age, size, or none of that."

"And neither do I," Noni stated, as she stepped forward with her fearless eyes fixed on Doony.

"Bitch, you better stay in your dike-ass lane! Before I slap the —"

14

Before his mouth could complete its statement, Noni came from the hip with a leaping left hook that powered off his electricity.

As the crowd shockingly stared down at Doony, who had blood trickling from the corner of his partially opened mouth, Lo-Lo grabbed her brother's hand and drug him along.

"Let's go!" Asha barked, grabbing Noni's shirt sleeve.

Snatching away, Noni swept the crowd with a photographic stare and warned, "If any one of y'all rat me out, I swear on my twin, I'ma do you much worse."

On account of her budding reputation, Noni's threat failed to fall on deaf ears.

With no way of knowing the extent of Doony's injury, Asha suggested they leave school early.

Once they had safely fled the building, Lo-Lo turned to question Noni in fascination, "Girl, how the fuck you put Doony to sleep like that?"

Noni reached in her coat pocket and withdrew a set of brass knuckles. "He was so busy running off at his mouth, that he ain't even see me slip these bitches on."

As they were laughing at Doony's misfortune, Lance stuck a hand inside his underwear.

"Look what I got!" he said.

All three girls were wide-eyed as they stared at the wad of money in his hand.

Recovering from her initial shock, Lo-Lo quickly pushed his hand downwards before scanning the area. "Boy, where'd you get that?"

"From Doony's locker."

"But I thought he caught you?"

Lance flashed a mischievous smile. "Nah, he thought he did but I had already got inside his locker. And when I seen him coming, I just hurried up and locked it back." He stopped to bend down and reach in his sock, from where he removed a small, square piece of aluminum. "There ain't a Master lock in school I can't open with one of these."

The girls could only shake their heads in awe and amusement, inwardly proud of Lance's courageous feat.

"Here, Noni," Lance said, offering her half of the money.

"I didn't mean to get you in trouble."

"Nah, you good, lil man," she playfully ruffled his hair.

"Because I had already been looking for a reason to expose his homophobic ass, anyway. So, if anything, I'm indebted to you."

After walking a few blocks over from the school building, the four folded themselves into a stolen Buick Regal. Noni reached beneath the driver seat and grabbed a 8-inch screwdriver, which she used to start the engine.

"Alright, put y'all mu'fucking seatbelts on," she jokingly ordered before speeding away from the curb.

Per Lance's request, they enjoyed a massive feast at a five-star restaurant and went to the movies. Then, as they were leaving the theatre later that evening, he slipped the remainder of his spoils into Lo-Lo's purse. With their mother being a full-fledge drug addict, he knew his sister could use the money for food and other household products.

After dropping Lo-Lo and Lance off at a small house on the west side, the twins took the interstate home.

It was a quarter to ten when Noni parked the car in an alleyway around the corner from their apartment complex.

After thoroughly cleansing the car's interior of their fingerprints, they marched in the direction of a housing project called The Brewster's.

Its murder rate at an all-time high, this was a complex hailed as a haven full of heathens, hustlers, and homicidal hooligans. A place where children as young as twelve could often be seen brandishing fully operable firearms as if they were mere water guns.

Acknowledging familiar faces as they stepped through the darkened complex, the twins approached the front door of their apartment and could hear loud music coming from inside. Because this was not uncommon, Asha inserted her key into the lock and they entered a real live nightmare.

"Get the fuck in here and shut the door!" barked a masked man, who was wielding a large revolver. While his identity was not yet known, but his name was Pee-Wee, and he was accompanied by his older brother, Otha, who gripped a sawed-off shotgun in steady hands.

Despite the fearful pounding of their teenage hearts, the twins calmly complied. To their horror, they saw their mother lying on the couch, bound and gagged. But worse, her right eye was swollen shut.

Like most women bred in the trenches of the inner city, their mother, Regina, was mainly attracted to men who led unlawful lifestyles. Presently involved with a drug dealer named Dullah, he controlled a large part of the city's marijuana and cocaine distribution. He used Regina's apartment as one of his stash houses, which was the cause of the current intrusion.

"Tie them hoes up," Pee-Wee ordered, as he stood near their mother in a wide-legged stance. He radiated an authoritative energy that implied he was in charge.

Moving with an efficiency that came from experience, Otha quickly subdued their hands and wrists before covering their mouths with a strip of duct tape.

Up until this point, Regina had managed to maintain her silence in regards to the location of the hidden drugs. But equally determined, Pee-Wee decided to change tactics.

Fully aware of Noni's sexual orientation, he ordered for Otha to remove her pants.

"I want you to show that lil bitch what she been missing out on," he cruelly encouraged him.

Asha began groaning in protest as Otha used his teeth to tear open an XL condom.

"You should've just gave it up," Pee-Wee coldly counseled Regina while caressing her cheek with the barrel of his revolver.

As Otha was on the verge of violating Noni's virginal womb, Asha attempted to break free.

"Bitch, you better be still," Pee-Wee warned as he went over to place a boot along Asha's spine. When she continued to violently struggle against the restraints, he snatched her head up from the floor and split the skin under her eye with the butt of his gun.

Flailing like a fish out of water, Noni went crazy at the sight of her sister being physically assaulted.

"You got the right one," Otha growled before delivering a vicious kick to Noni's kidney.

When Noni rolled over in pain, Otha slammed the shotgun down on her mouth, knocking out her two front teeth.

"Now, move again and I'll crush your sister's skull," he warned, then turned Noni her back on her stomach.

As blood was leaking from Asha's face and onto the floor, she helplessly stared into her twin's tormented eyes.

"I'm so sorry, Noni," she silently whimpered.

With each of the predator's painful thrusts, the temperature of Noni's heart drastically declined. This was a horrid experience from which she would never fully recover.

Once finished with his perverted performance, Otha then went to stand over Asha; his sheathed penis coated in blood.

"You ready to talk now?" Pee-Wee questioned Regina, "Or should he get started on your favorite one?"

Tears were streaming from her good eye as she slowly bobbed her head in defeat. She loved Dullah with all her

18

heart, but she couldn't bear to see both girls be defiled in the most demeaning way.

After removing pounds of marijuana and cocaine from inside an attic, Otha hurriedly descended the stairs and gave his brother a confirmatory nod.

Swiveling on his heels, Pee-Wee went into the kitchen and opened the refrigerator. Grabbing a bottle of Gatorade, he poured out its contents while walking back to the front room.

Regina looked up as he inserted the barrel into the bottle's opening. Knowing she was only moments away from meeting her maker, she closed her eyes and prayed in advance. "Lord, please watch over my girls. I know I didn't set a good example, but please don't hold them accountable for my mis –"

Pee-Wee silenced her supplication with several muffled shots.

Once the two monsters had fled out the back door, Asha wiggled over to her sister, whose face was frozen into a callous expression.

Placing her head within inches of Noni's, Asha returned her stare and slowly nodded. For she both knew and agreed with what her twin was thinking...

"We can't live until them niggas is dead!"

Chapter 3

It was in the evening hours, when a '72 Pontiac GTO turned into a scrapyard and sped through a maze of inoperative vehicles. As the GTO braked before a garage-like structure, the driver side window lowered and Noni stuck her head out, lifting it at a small camera that was undoubtedly being monitored.

Seconds later, the garage door began to mechanically raise and Noni drove inside.

Housing a collection of cars that ranged from muscle to modern, this was the secretive site of the city's most lucrative chop shops. So, in spite of the hour, there were a number of people presently at work.

Exiting the GTO in dark clothing, Noni and Asha were acknowledged by several employees.

"Boss man in the office," a man named Rome said, as he busied himself beneath the hood of a Mercedes Benz truck.

With Asha in the lead, the twins climbed a metal staircase and came upon a closed door, on which Asha knocked twice before turning its knob.

Settled behind a desk was a muscular-built man with a hairless head, piercing dark eyes, and the full beard of a devout Muslim. Along with a dual set of tattooed teardrops that tallied his number of kills and losses, he had the presence of a predator who was primed to pounce.

Ending a phone call as they entered the room, he rose to smilingly greet them with handshakes. "How's my two lil murder mamas?"

While the gesture was subtle, he held on to Asha's hand a second longer than was necessary. But a relationship outside of business was repulsive in her eyes. Because not only was he out of her age range, but he was an ex-lover of their late mother's.

After instructing the twins to take a seat, Dullah approached a mini refrigerator and asked them if they wanted a drink.

"We good," Asha spoke up.

Pouring himself a generous amount of Cognac, Dullah retook his seat behind the desk and flashed a knowing grin. "I see somebody handled their business at Belle Isle the other day."

"Sometimes foul shit happens to foul mu'fuckas," Noni simply replied.

While the twins knew he'd love to personally hear how they gunned down the men responsible for their mother's death and the theft of his drugs, they also knew better than to volunteer any incriminating information. Other than themselves and Lo-Lo, they lent their trust to no one else. And besides, the killing had been committed on a separate basis.

Slightly offended by their secretive stance, Dullah scoffed at Noni's comment. "Y'all act like it wasn't because of me you were able to take care of that."

"And you act like what's understood needs to be explained," Noni spat right back.

Dullah held her gaze for a second before he nodded his head and smiled. "Yeah, you absolutely right. Silly me."

He then reached in a drawer of his desk and removed a small piece of paper, which he held out to Asha. "I need these before Sunday."

Asha leaned forward to accept it. "With all due respect, Dullah, we feel it's time you gave us a bigger role. We've been working for you for two years now, so our loyalty is unquestionable. And we'll be twenty-one this summer, so we trying to enter womanhood with at least six-figures in our bank account."

Draining his drink in one gulp, he sat the glass aside and peered deeply into Asha's eyes. "I mean, clearly you've given this some thought. So tell me, what exactly do you have in mind?"

"We was thinking the weed game. We gotta enough money saved up to cop a few pounds, and you could front us just as many. Everybody and they mama smoke bud, so it wouldn't be a problem getting it gone. And it's less risks involved."

Dullah barely pondered over her proposal before he began shaking his head. "Nah, I don't think that's a good idea. Because it would attract too many thirsty ass niggas. I ain't saying y'all couldn't hold it down, but you'd have to prove yourselves on a constant basis. And excessive violence ain't never been good for business."

"Dullah, we appreciate you giving us a lane," Asha persisted, "But we've outgrown it. And besides, the rewards just ain't worth the risks no more. We need something bigger than stealing cars."

"Tell you what. I can probably put you in line for some driving work. You'll get like five thousand a haul. Do it twice a month... and you do the math."

Knowing he was referring to hauling drugs up and down the interstate, Asha scoffed. "Yeah, and you do the math on how much time we'll get if they pull us over. Snitching ain't in our blood, so we'd be old ladies by the time we got out."

"Dullah, why you trying to play us like we on some corny shit out here?" Noni cut in, having held her tongue for as long as possible. "I'm saying, you acting like –"

Asha gave her a subtle headshake, which Noni ignored. "Nah, fuck that, twin. This nigga act like we a pair of lames, or something. Like we supposed to be his pawns until he decide otherwise. Nigga, we ain't Regina."

"Noni, you need to put some respect on that shit, for real," Dullah growled. "Because I ain't gon' sit here and listen to you speak ill of the dead. Especially, when it's toward a woman I once loved."

Noni smirked. "Yeah, I guess you would feel that way about a woman who loved you more than her own child."

While the twins had only voiced their opinion to one another, they held their mother accountable for what happened to Noni. Because had she given the intruders the location of the drugs when they initially asked, then they wouldn't have been forced to resort to such barbaric measures. But Asha was disappointed in her sister for allowing emotion to override wisdom. Because now, Dullah was awakened to the presence of a hidden animosity.

"I don't know what that's supposed to mean," Dullah said, standing up from the desk. "But you way out of pocket, Noni. So, I'ma have to ask you to leave my office."

"Gladly," she replied, springing from her chair with a scowl of contempt.

As Asha rose to join her sister, Dullah asked if they could have a word alone.

"Not if it's about my sister."

"I promise you it ain't."

When Asha whispered for her sister to step out, Noni loudly sighed and exited the room, careful to slam the door as hard as she could.

Dullah closed his eyes and inhaled a calming breath.

"What's up?" Asha asked, interrupting his thoughts of strangling Noni. "What you want to holler at me about?"

He closed the distance between them and laid his hands on both of her shoulders. "I've been in these streets a lot longer than you, Asha. Which means I've seen and experienced twice as much, if not more. So, trust me when I tell you I've seen plenty of women with plenty of potential sneaking out of soup kitchens. Because without the proper resources, aspirations ain't nothing more than farfetched dreams. I'd hate to see you get stuck in the same boat," he continued in an earnest tone. "So take advantage of your resources and let me help you. Let me groom you into the woman you're supposed to be. And watch that bank account grow faster than a newborn baby."

Although she maintained a neutral expression, Asha was inwardly laughing in mockery at Dullah's spiel. He was a pitiful excuse for a man. And it was in that moment when she realized that unless she gave in to his indecent desires, he'd never promote them above their present position.

"Don't take this offensive, Dullah," she said, gently removing his hands from her shoulders. "But there could never be anything more than business between us. And it ain't that you unattractive, or nothing like that. But it's the whole fact that you was fucking on my mama. So, if I gotta go against morals to get ahead, then I guess I'ma die on some broke ass shit."

When Asha blew out the office and descended the stairs, an inquisitive Noni was on her heels. "What that nigga want with you, love?"

It wasn't until they reentered the car did Asha answer. "Basically, we ain't getting promoted unless I give him some pussy."

"What?" Noni exclaimed, reaching beneath her seat to snatch up a chrome revolver. "I'll blow that nigga shit off his muthafucking shoulders!"

Asha roughly grabbed her arm, "Get control of your emotions, girl. I only told you what it is because you my sister. But don't expose our hands again, like you did earlier. And besides, one monkey don't stop no whole fucking show. Now, put that gun up and get us the fuck out of here."

Dullah was watching from his office window as the GTO reversed out the garage. His pride wounded by the molars of rejection, he couldn't refrain from biting back. But he'd do so in a manner where it would affect both sisters.

Once the car was gone, he yelled down for Rome, whom he had recently appointed as the shop's manager.

Rome bounded the stairs two at a time. "What's good, boss?"

"The twins gon' be bringing a few cars through here sometime this week. But when they do, I want you to tell them they got the years wrong, and you can't do nothing with 'em. When they put up a fuss, offer them half, and nothing more."

Despite his puzzlement over the request, Rome knew better than to pry and shrugged in consent. "Alright, whatever you say."

"Oh, and Rome," Dullah called out as he turned to leave, "Be sure to put that other half in your back pocket."

Rome beamed in response; his confusion quickly cured by the mention of extra money.

Closing the shop down around midnight, Dullah folded his burly frame inside a late model Dodge Ram. Before exiting the garage, he reached over to unlock the glovebox and grabbed a fully loaded firearm. He kept a low profile, but a highly cautious nature.

Dullah's eyes were glued to his rearview as he turned down the suburban street on which he resided. Though he was careful to rotate routes to his residence, one in his position could never be overly wary. As a native of a city known for its unforgivable violence and betrayal, he knew the simplest safety precautions would often prevent the severest situations.

Slyly shielding the semi along his left leg as he entered the house, Dullah was on the verge of deactivating the alarm, when he felt a presence behind him and tensed up.

"We tend to be so worried about what's behind us," a voice said near his ear, "That we can be oblivious to what's already in front."

When Dullah slowly turned around, he was presented with a picture of chocolate perfection.

"You like a fucking cat, you know that?" he smiled, pulling Unique forward by the belt of her overcoat.

"Yeah, well, I need you to be a dog on this pussy tonight," she replied, then untied the coat to expose her symmetrical nakedness.

Detecting a sliver of sadness in Unique's slanted eyes, Dullah cupped her chin and inquired, "What's wrong?"

She averted her gaze. "Nothing I can't handle."

"That ain't what I asked you. Now, tell me who did what, so I can make arrangements for their death."

Allured by his aggressive nature, and fully aware of his reach in the streets, Unique revealed, "Somebody killed my peoples over the weekend. And we was super close, so me and my sister lightweight fucked up behind it."

"You ain't talking about that demo at Belle Isle, is you?"

She nodded.

"Them was your peoples?" Dullah asked in genuine surprise.

Unique looked up with a frown. "Yeah, why you say it like that?"

He obviously couldn't inform her of his involvement, so he quickly responded, "Nah, it's just that I heard that was on some personal shit. So until you find out who did it, you might want to be a lil more mindful of your movements out here. But now that I know them was your peeps, I'ma definitely keep my ear to the streets and tell you if I hear something."

"I'd appreciate it," Unique nodded, encircling her arms around his neck. "But right now I don't want to think about all that, Dullah. I just want you to take me upstairs and fuck me to sleep."

Eager to oblige, he swept Unique off her feet and carried her up the steps.

In light of the new and useful information in relation to the double murder, a poisonous plot had already developed in Dullah's viperous mind. So if Asha didn't soon submit to his earlier proposal, then he'd have no choice but to inform Unique of the killers responsible for her peoples death.

Upstairs in his bedroom, Dullah was fulfilling Unique's wishes while she clawed at his back and demanded he dig deeper. Had her eyes been opened, she would've noticed he was watching her with a weird expression. For Dullah was digging into Unique's orifice but staring at the face of Asha.

Chapter 4

Over half-eaten breakfast sandwiches, Asha was quietly addressing Noni and Lo-Lo as they sat around a corner table in McDonald's.

"We've struggled long enough," Asha said, jabbing her index finger on the table for emphasis. "And if we expect to get any further than where we're at, then we gon' have to be twice as vicious as these clowns out here controlling the streets. What we want is what we'll have to take. Simple as that."

Lo-Lo nodded in full agreement, "I'm all in, love. Because it's a fact that they can't outthink us. But we as women have been playing the background for so long, that they done forgot who really keep this bitch spinning. And it's time we reminded 'em."

Also twenty years of age, Lo-Lo was presently employed as an exotic dancer at one of the liveliest strip clubs in Detroit. While it paid the bills and enabled her to maintain a well-kept appearance, the girl was actually struggling to keep her head above water. And if she had any plans on boarding the boat-of-life, which the underprivileged often missed, then it was no secret that she'd have to adopt an ambition far above average.

"I still can't believe the audacity of that nigga, Dullah," Noni chimed in. "He been paying us pennies on the dollar for the past two years, and not once have we brought him any complaints. But the minute we -"

"Fuck Dullah!" Asha cut her off. "He just showed us who he really is. And now that he's taken off his mask, we just gotta make sure we don't let him put it back on. So from now on, let his name taste like dog shit in our mouths. He gets no more of our energy. And like Lo-Lo said, we gon' show his clown-ass that this a woman's world for real."

Dropping her voice to a secretive tone, Asha leaned forward and began to outline the first step they'd take toward the site of success. And unbeknownst to Dullah, he'd play a major role in their initial movement.

Noni and Lo-Lo were all smiles while listening to Asha's plan. And this was an instance when they'd take considerable joy in biting the hand that had once fed them.

"...Because we already know it take money to make money," Asha continued. "So once we build up our bank from this lil' move right here, then we can begin the construction of our empire; brick-by-brick. And in the words of that lame whose name we no longer speak, watch our bank accounts grow faster than newborn babies."

Ecstatic by the exactness of Asha's plan, Lo-Lo smilingly pointed an accusing finger at her, "Girl, you been thinking on this for a minute. With your little ruthless ass!"

"I have," she admitted. "But there's only one problem."

Noni frowned, "And what's that?"

"Behind a move like this, we gon' need some serious artillery. So unless one of y'all got a gun connect I don't know about, then we gotta figure out how to survive long enough to get from point A to B."

Noni had a circle of savages she often hung around, but none of whom would have access to the amount of artillery to which Asha was referring to. And Lo-Lo would arouse unwanted suspicion were she to make such a felonious inquiry.

As they were pondering over a solution to their problem, Lo-Lo glanced at the time and jumped up from the table.

"Shit!" she cursed, reaching for her jacket and purse, "I'ma fuck around and be late. I'll see y'all later on tonight."

"Be careful, love," Asha said as they quickly hugged.

Shortly after they watched Lo-Lo take off in the Tahoe, Noni received a text message from a young felon named

Teer. At only 16-years-old, he was fully responsible for the fulfilment of their business deal with Dullah.

"Come on, we gotta roll," she said, texting him a reply, "Our lil' demon on deck."

***

The twins pulled behind an abandoned power plant, where two cars were already present, one a bucket and the other a beauty.

As they parked alongside a pearl-green convertible and hopped out, Teer unfolded himself from behind the coupe's wheel with an infectious smile. "What's up with the mob?"

Boyishly handsome, the caramel complected teen sported short dreads over a hairless face and mischievous eyes. And though he measured only 5'5", his sizable heart supplemented his stunted stature.

"Boy, you did your thang!" Noni commended as she approvingly eyed the '63 Corvette. With its chrome wheels and flip-up headlights, the split-window coupe was undoubtedly worth over $100,000.

"I was out scouting all morning," Teer grinned, pleased by her praise. "Then, I caught an old head cranking this bitch up in his garage. I told him he could die for it or live without it. But either way, he was losing it."

Asha removed a small bankroll from her pocket and paid him for his services. "Try to spend your money wisely, Teer. Because after you get them other two cars, we killing that contract. And I can't say how long it'll be before I can put food on your plate."

"Why, what's going on?"

"Simply put, we taking too many risks for not nearly enough money. I know because of your age they wouldn't crack down too hard on you if you was to ever get caught but fuck all that. If we gon' be out in the middle of a ocean, then it damn sure shouldn't be on no fucking rafter. So we about to build our own shit and catch our own fish. And if niggas don't like it, then we skinning they ass too."

"Ooh, you talking about a takeover!" Teer exclaimed, his eyes lighting up with excitement. "Y'all ready to get on some mob shit for real. Yeah, you can most definitely count me in! Matter fact," he added, withdrawing the money from his pocket and handing it back to Asha. "You can keep that shit."

Shaking her head in refusal, Asha smiled at his sincerity. "Nah, you good, Teer. That's you."

"Man, I'm straight," he persisted, forcing Asha to take back the money. "So, consider this and my next two payments as contributions to the cause. And besides, I got faith in y'all. So I already know that lil' shit come back a thousand times over."

Deeply impressed by his visionary perspective, Asha and Noni were grateful to have someone like Teer on their team. In fact, it was his recurrent displays of loyalty that led to them regarding him as the little brother they never had. So they'd care for and protect him as if he was of their DNA.

As Noni slipped on a pair of baseball gloves, which faithfully hung from the back pockets of her pants, Teer had a sudden thought that made his eyes widen.

"Damn, I almost forgot to tell y'all," he excitedly announced. "My big cousin coming home next week. He did like four in I-Max. And I know y'all don't be fucking with niggas all like that, but cuz action packed. Like, on some Navy Seal shit. And he loyal. So with what y'all talking about doing, he'd be perfect. And y'all probably heard of him."

Upon hearing his name, their eyebrows rose in genuine surprise, as he was certainly someone they'd heard about on numerous occasions. The most notable tale was of him chipping his front tooth while in the line of duty. It was reported that he had suffered a gunshot wound to his arm during a deadly shootout. With the need to reload, but having the use of only one arm, he allegedly used his mouth to feed a bullet into the gun's chamber.

The twins exchanged a brief glance, both thinking along the same lines. They definitely needed the manpower, and his cousin was rumored to have filled up a small cemetery.

After informing Teer that they'd accompany him on the trip to I-Max the following week, Noni grabbed a ski mask and gun from her car.

"Aye, yo, you check this nigga?" she asked Teer, rolling the mask down over her face.

Assuring he had, Noni popped the trunk of the Corvette - where an older man was curled inside the cramped enclosure.

"Please, don't kill me," he whimpered, placing his hands before his face in a protective gesture.

Noni ordered for him to climb out and lay face down on the ground.

Once he complied, she threatened, "If you move an inch before you count to a hundred, you gon' die right here on this concrete, all alone."

To prevent the car theft victims from immediately calling the police, Teer was instructed to bring them along. Then, once the group gathered in a location that was usually in the vicinity of Dullah's shop, they'd let the person go unharmed. And by the time they reached a phone, Noni would have delivered the car and collected a $3,000 payment.

Inside the 'Vette, Noni laid the pistol on the passenger seat before connecting her phone to the car's customized radio. This being a habit of hers, she'd select a certain song to enhance the experience.

With Future boasting on the visibility of his chain behind 5% tint, Noni threw the shifter in drive and smashed the gas. Snatching off her mask as the coupe exited the lot with a piercing scream, she had no way of knowing that they were on the verge of being swindled.

Chapter 5

Parked outside a one story building in Milan, Michigan, Lo-Lo was periodically scanning her surroundings as she inserted compressed balloons inside her vaginal cavity. Each balloon containing a cheap strand of tobacco, she was minutes away from conveying a quarter pound of it into a Federal prison.

Exiting the truck with confidence, despite the nervous pounding of her heart, Lo-Lo donned a pair of designer shades and marched towards the front entrance.

It was a Saturday afternoon, which meant the visiting room would be packed. And also working to her advantage was the form fitting jeans that showcased a bottom some believed to be bought. With the visits being supervised by mainly male guards, she'd exploit their weakness by using her voluptuous figure as a visual distraction.

After presenting her ID and a phony smile to an employee at the front desk, Lo-Lo was unsuspectingly admitted into the visiting room.

With her blonde curls cascading over her shoulders and back, she swaggered towards a table for two, well aware of the ogling stares her presence elicited. This was one white girl who was cold enough to pose among the coldest.

Paying little attention to the reckless eyeballing from several thirsty inmates, Lo-Lo kept her focus on the door through which her visitor would enter the room.

Her patience paid off moments later, when the door opened and Lance's face came into view.

"Hey, sis!" her little brother beamed, gripping her in a bear hug. "I was scared you wouldn't make it."

"Boy, only God could've stopped me from coming," she earnestly assured him. "Although, I will admit that I was damn near late."

Before taking a seat, she asked him what he wanted to eat. "And I brought like fifty, so you can get whatever you want."

Naming a number of items, mainly junk food, Lance lowered his head as she went to the vending machines. For he had no desire to watch his sister be visually undressed by half the visiting room.

Lance was nibbling on a chicken sandwich, when he casually questioned, "Did you bring that?"

Lo-Lo nodded, taking a sip of her bottled water.

"Do you still remember what to do?"

Again, she nodded.

After a moment of studying her little brother's appearance with an eye of appraisal, Lo-Lo leaned forward to quietly address him.

"What's going on, Lance?" she inquired, referring to the reason behind his request for the tobacco. "Because I know you don't smoke. And you're definitely not a dealer."

His chewing slowed, "It's not my fault, sis. I swear it ain't."

"Alright, just tell me what happened."

Taking a deep breath, Lance went on to explain how he'd been in the shower, when a sock wrapped package was thrown inside. Not knowing who had threw it or what was in it, he quickly dried off and got out the shower, leaving the sock on the floor.

Several days later, two men approached him as he was leaving the chow hall. They claimed to have received a note from their friend in the hole, who told them he'd ditched the package off on Lance while being pursued by a guard. Lance had confirmed that that was true, but said he'd left the sock in the shower, as he had no idea of what was going on. Accused of either being a liar, or the dumbest honkey on earth, he was ordered to reimburse them for the lost package. And a failure to do so would result in a vicious beating. Without a fighter's spirit or an ally's assistance, Lance saw compliance as his only option.

Angered by someone taking advantage of her brother's timid nature, Lo-Lo glared around the visiting room, wondering if either of the bullies were present.

"Where these dudes from?" she asked Lance.

"I think Flint. Why?"

"Because once you give this to them, it won't end there. They'll see you as an opportunity. If you can get it once, you can get it again."

"So what should I do?" Lance worriedly inquired.

"Don't worry, I'ma take care of it. But I need you to get me their whole names, and their prison numbers, if possible."

"What you gon' do?"

"Oh, I don't know," Lo-Lo casually shrugged. "Maybe tell Noni that somebody in here fucking with her little buddy."

Lance's eyes grew wide with hope. "Noni don't play."

Smiling, Lo-Lo shook her head. "Especially not when it come to you. So I just need you to stay safe until we can straighten this out."

More like her son than brother, Lo-Lo blamed herself for Lance's incarceration. Because had she been there to watch over him, he wouldn't have thought robbing a federal bank was his only means of survival. But as a result of her and the twins doing a bid themselves, her naive brother had been convinced by an alleged friend to accompany him on a botched robbery, for which he had received a sixty-month sentence.

Observing Lance with a tender expression as he resumed eating his food, Lo-Lo was thinking of how she'd do whatever it took to protect her brother. And if they could trade places, she'd change clothes without a moment's hesitation.

Lance caught her watching him and awkwardly grinned, "What?"

"Nothing," Lo-Lo smiled. "Just thinking about how much I love you, that's all."

"I love you, too, sis."

Lo-Lo looked away, forcing herself not to tear up. Now was not the time to be emotional, especially in front of Lance. She needed to be a symbol of strength and support.

"I'll be alright, Loretta," Lance said, addressing his sister by her government name. "I know you be blaming yourself, but it's not your fault that I'm in here. I made a stupid mistake. And as long as I don't get in trouble, I'll be out in just three more years."

Appreciative of his attempt at consoling her, Lo-Lo reached over to grasp his hand. "You're a real angel, brother. So I don't doubt God gon' watch over one of his own. But as your sister, I'ma still do everything I can to make your bid as comfortable as possible. And I didn't want to tell you yet, but I think Asha done figured it out. So, we shouldn't be struggling much longer."

Mindful of the time, as her Lance reminisced on better days, Lo-Lo excused herself from the table at exactly an hour prior to when visits ended. Along the way to the restroom, she purposely locked eyes with an inmate who'd been aiming desiring looks in direction throughout the entire visit. With neatly kept dreads and a full beard, he appeared to be in his late thirties.

Exiting the restroom minutes later, Lo-Lo slyly glanced at the guards before stopping at her admirer's table. Joined by a younger version of himself, his well-dressed visitor had to be either his son or sibling.

"You know me?" she flirtatiously inquired of the older man.

"Nah, but I'd like to," he replied with direct eye contact.

Lo-Lo smirked, then nudged her head at Lance. "Do you know him?"

He glanced over at Lance before shaking his head, "I've seen him around, but we've never met."

"Yeah, well, that's my little brother. And if a person don't like him, then they can't possibly like me."

When Lo-Lo returned to the table, Lance leaned forward and nervously rattled off, "Sis, what are you doing? Do you know who that man that is?"

"Nah, who is he?"

"That's Monster. He basically runs this whole compound. He can get a man murdered with just snap of his fingers."

Grateful for following her intuition, Lo-Lo smiled, "Well, then, trust me, bro, I don't think you'll have nothing to worry about. In fact, don't be surprised if he start being nice to you."

Lo-Lo knew that if you gave a wishful man just the slightest glimpse of hope, he'd go above and beyond to make a further impression. And in this instance, his efforts would work in Lance's favor.

When a guard loudly announced that visiting hours were over, Lo-Lo and Lance slowly rose to their feet. Though they knew the moment would eventually arrive, saying goodbye was the most difficult part of their visits.

"I took care of that," she whispered in his ear as they tightly embraced. "So that'll give me enough time to handle that other situation."

Swallowing a lump in his throat, Lance just bobbed his head in response. Had they been alone, he would've cried on her shoulder and begged her not to leave him in that animalistic environment.

Lo-Lo pried their bodies apart and held him firmly by the arms. "I failed you once, but it won't happen again. So don't worry, Lance. And I'ma put some money in your account when I get back to the city, so you'll be able to go to commissary next week. Okay?"

"Okay," he nodded. This time with a bit of enthusiasm. Anyone that knew Lance, knew that he loved food.

"I love you, brother."

"I love you, too."

Before she broke down herself, Lo-Lo kissed his cheek and gently pushed him in the direction of his exit.

Lance paused in the doorway and turned to offer a subtle wave.

Lo-Lo patted her hand over her heart in a gesture of affection.

As she was gathering her things, she felt the intensity of someone's gaze and looked over to lock eyes with the man they called Monster. Though there was no verbal exchange, she could easily see the desire in his stare. So she slipped him a wink before exiting the room.

Lo-Lo was locking in her seatbelt, when a black Audi pulled alongside her. Inside the car was Monster's visitor, who motioned for her to lower her window.

When she complied, he asked, "Where you from, my baby?"

Lo-Lo smiled at his dialect before answering, "I'm from the 'D'."

"Oh, yeah?" he lifted his eyebrows. "Me too. So shid, shoot me your number so we can link up, you feel me?"

"Maybe next time."

"Well, hopefully I'll see you around then." He smiled, then sped off with a loud squeal.

"Men ain't shit." Lo-Lo smirked to herself as she threw the Tahoe in drive.

Chapter 6

In pursuit of a bachelor's degree in business management, Asha was presently planted in a classroom of Wayne State. Although her accountant teacher spoke in a clear tone, she didn't hear a word of what was said. With her mind consumed by the pieces of her daring plan, she had to ensure that the puzzle was perfectly put together, as the lives of her and her loved ones literally depended on it.

After a heated exchange with Rome at the chop shop, where the twins declined to accept one silver dime, Asha saw the incident as a sign that her plans were in line with a higher divinity. For she truly believed that costly adversity usually preceded richly success. It all boiled down to a person's endurance.

At the end of class, Asha was placing her books in her backpack, when she was approached by an attractive classmate. Aware of him harboring a secret crush on her, she was mildly surprised that he'd finally found the nerve to step forward.

"Excuse my intrusion," he stated in a serious tone, "But I think you should know that they gotta warrant out for your arrest."

Asha frowned. "A warrant?"

He nodded in confirmation.

"For what?" she asked, her mind racing and heart pounding.

"First-degree burglary."

"Burglary?" she repeated in disbelief.

"Yup. About a month ago, when the semester first started, you broke into my mind and stole my heart. And since I didn't know how else to get it back, I had to press charges."

Exhaling in relief, Asha laughingly pushed him. "Boy, you almost scared me to death! You had me thinking they might've confused me with somebody else."

"Nah, but seriously though," he said, "I have been thinking about you since the first day I saw you. And I'm sure you already know, but you on some gorgeous shit."

On this particular day, she was indeed looking considerably cute with her crinkled hair, cotton candy lip gloss, and curvy figure stretching the seams of a Jordan jumpsuit.

"Thank you," Asha smiled at his compliment. "And you ain't too bad looking yourself."

He laughed, "Alright, I'll accept that."

Extending a hand that bore clean fingernails, he introduced himself as Jaylen.

"I'm Asha," she replied, surprising him with a firm shake.

"Well, Asha, can I walk you to your next class?"

"I don't know about that. Not after that stunt you just pulled."

"Tell you what. You let me walk with you and I'll drop all charges."

Playing along, Asha acted as if she was giving serious thought to his request before finally voicing her consent. "Alright, but you better drop 'em as soon as you leave here."

They exchanged basic conversation during the short trip to her next class.

"So, how do you feel about giving me your phone number?" Jaylen smiled. "Or you could just take mines if that makes you feel more comfortable."

Asha didn't doubt that Jaylen was a decent dude, but right now the timing was off. She was about to embark on a journey that required full focus and minimal distractions. So any emotional attachments were temporarily out of the picture.

Lightly touching his forearm, Asha let him down easy. "You definitely came with a different approach. I underestimated you. But to keep it a buck, right now isn't a good time for me to be establishing new friendships. But who knows, maybe our paths will cross somewhere later in life."

Not easily deterred, Jaylen scribbled something on a piece of paper and held it out to her.

"What's this?" she asked, hesitantly accepting it.

"My number. Maybe one day you'll decide to use it, or maybe you won't. But in my world, the glass is always half full."

Impressed by his optimistic outlook, Asha thanked him for his company, then left him spellbound by a departing view of her inflated bottom.

***

A sizable crowd was attentively assembled around a boxing ring at a local gym.

Wearing headgear and gloves, the two contenders in the ring were engaged in an intense sparring match. Whereas one was dark complected and stockily built, the other was light skin and covered in colorful ink.

"Noni, quit dropping your hands!" her coach yelled from a corner of the ring.

Despite going against a bigger opponent, Noni couldn't refrain from emulating the showy style of her favorite fighter, Roy Jones Jr.

Aggressive by nature, Noni had been hanging around boxing gyms since she was a little girl. She not only saw the sport as a means of protecting herself and sister, but she was fascinated by the graceful footwork, automated reflexes, and precise hand speed. While other children were watching cartoons, she'd been studying film on Roy Jones.

Inside the ring, Noni was showcasing her slip game as she easily evaded a number of swings from her frustrated opponent. Then, in a sudden conversion, she switched to offense and delivered a crisp combo that connected with his head and body.

As she had him pent in a corner, digging into his midsection with shoveling hooks, her coach blew a whistle and announced that the session was over.

There was a round of applause as Noni and her opponent shook hands in good sportsmanship. And though they were both from the same gym, majority of the spectators were in support of her. Because she not only possessed an impressive swag, but it was uncommon to see a girl her age with such an exceptional boxing skill and IQ.

"When you gon' start taking your gift more seriously?" her coach inquired while removing her gloves. Having been in the sport for decades, there wasn't a doubt in his mind that Noni would go pro if she was fully committed.

"As soon as I can afford to," she answered, pulling off her headgear. "Because trust me, coach, there ain't too much I love more than being in this ring. But right now I gotta help my sister figure some shit out."

"But, Noni, I told you I'd help if you promise to be dedicated. Don't you know how much money you'd be making if you went pro? You'd be able to take care of your sister, and whoever else you decided to."

A disbeliever of free generosity, Noni declined his offer for the hundredth time. "It's cool, coach. We gon' figure it out. And if you feel you wasting your time, then I understand. But I gotta do what's best for me and my twin."

Without giving him a chance to reply, Noni climbed out the ring and joined the group of people who were waiting to praise her for an entertaining performance.

As Noni's coach was observing her with a saddened expression, he was wondering what experience had caused her to be so wary of men. With an eye for greatness, which rarely came along, he could only pray that his prodigy would tap into her talent before it was ultimately too late.

Pulling into the Brewster projects, where a crowd of criminals were noisily loitering, Noni double parked the GTO and hopped out.

"What's up with the Mob?" several men sang in unison as Noni walked up. With a lively energy and a Spartan's spirit, her presence was always welcomed.

"What's good wit' it?" she smiled, offering handshakes to only a selected few.

Taking offense at being overlooked, there was a clown in the crowd who was eyeballing Noni with a sour expression. Recently paroled from a six year bid in prison, he'd reentered society with a tough man's mentality.

"What you niggas on?" Noni inquired, as she noticed their attention was drawn to the screen of someone's phone.

"We watching that Belle Isle shit," a man named Pierre answered. Originally from the Brewster's himself, Pierre was known for knowing about everything that went on in the city.

"That Belle Isle shit?"

They made room for her in the huddle and Noni saw to her surprise that they were watching a recording of the double murder for which her and Asha were responsible.

Noni masked her shock with a question, "Where the fuck y'all get this at?"

Pierre answered that it had been posted on Facebook earlier that day.

"Man, look how he stomped that nigga head in!" one man pointed out in glorification.

"Fuck all that," countered another observer. "Look how he stepped on that other nigga's neck and emptied the clip in his shit. Boy, I ain't seen John Wick put down no move like that."

As Noni listened to them excitedly highlight their favorite parts, she couldn't help but feel a sense of supremacy.

Because they had no idea that the goblin they glorified was standing right in their presence.

With his arms crossed and a toothpick dangling from a corner of his mouth, the parolee was leaning against a car as he glared at Noni on the sly. She had rubbed him the wrong way, and he thirsted for a reason to publicly reprove her.

In tune with her senses, Noni felt someone staring and turned to lock eyes with the glaring parolee. Normally, she'd ignore such a trivial thing, but the fact that she'd caught him in the act of staring was an issue that had to be addressed.

"What's good, bruh?" Noni asked with a lift of her head. "You got something on your mind?"

The tone of her inquiry caused everyone to tune in. They were clueless as to what had transpired, but it wasn't a mystery that Noni loved to fight. And she preferred male opponents... of all sizes.

Known as Diesel, the parolee uncrossed his massive arms and rose up off the car. "I'm saying, who the fuck is you to question what's on my mind? Clearly, you don't know who the fuck I am!"

"Clearly, I don't give a fuck," Noni retorted. "But if I was to guess, I'd say you some tough ass, buff ass nigga that just came home on some broke ass shit."

Heated by the eruption of laughter, as well as the accuracy of her theory, Diesel clenched his fists and hissed, "Bitch, I'll treat you like the man you portraying to be and break all your shit."

"Bitch?" Noni repeated, as if that was the only word of his threat that registered. "Yeah, you clearly don't know who the fuck I am, either," she continued, pulling her hoodie over her head and handing her phone to Pierre. "Because a nigga ain't never called Noni no bitch and didn't go to sleep right afterwards."

When she slipped in a mouthpiece, which lived in her sports bra, then removed the baseball gloves from her back pocket, Diesel looked around in amusement.

"Is this a joke?"

"You 'bout to find out," one man knowingly smiled, anxious to see Noni in action.

"Man, I'm finna... " as Diesel went to step towards Noni, he was grabbed by his friend who was responsible for bringing him around.

"Let that lil shit go, my baby," he duly advised. "It ain't even that serious."

Diesel screwed up his face, to which his friend quietly replied, "It ain't worth it, bro, trust me. That ain't the average girl."

While Noni being a fighter was factual, she was also suspected by many of being a sniper.

"Watch out," Diesel snatched his arm away. "You niggas out here fooling. Somebody should've been put this lil pretty bitch in her place."

As the two were on the verge of squaring off, Pierre informed Noni that her sister was calling. Had it been anyone else, he would've pressed decline.

She reluctantly spit out her mouthpiece and took the call. "Yeah, what up?"

"Why the fuck is you answering the phone like I'm bothering you, or something?" Asha snapped on the other end. "What you got going on?"

"Ain't nothing," Noni answered, walking out of earshot.

"Girl, don't lie to me. Now, what the fuck you got going on, Noni?"

"This nigga called me a bitch and I'm 'bout to beat his ass."

"Yeah, well, not before you come pick me up from school. You was supposed to be here ten minutes ago."

"Aw, damn, twin," Noni groaned in guilt. "That's my fault. I cold forgot. I'm on my way right now. I'm sorry."

Disconnecting the call, Noni promised Diesel that they would revisit this matter at a later time. "...Because we definitely gotta catch that round."

"Anytime," he replied, making the fatal mistake of minimizing a woman's capabilities.

Because had Diesel been familiar with how the animal kingdom operated, he would've known that it were the female lions who carried out the hunting.

Chapter 7

Wearing protective glasses and earplugs, the twins stood beside each other in a gun range, firing at paper targets that hung thirty yards away. With fake ID's verifying they were legally of age, this was something they did on a monthly basis.

After clearing two ten round clips in a matter of seconds, they pressed a button to retract their targets. Both sheets bore a number of holes in the center area. Pleased at their collective accuracy, they replaced the sheets and repeated the process.

"So, who was this boy you got into with?" Asha finally inquired as they were wrapping up their session. She'd been upset over Noni's tardiness and had spoken very little since being picked up from school.

"I don't know," Noni shrugged, "Some big ass bully who just got out."

"What happened?"

"I mean, I was chilling with the homies, then I looked up and the nigga was just staring at me. And when I addressed it, he got straight on some Randy Savage type shit. I ain't never seen this nigga a day in my life, so I don't know where all that animosity came from."

Asha wore a thoughtful expression as they exited the facility. With an aim to erect an empire in the heart of a heartless region, she knew the importance of establishing and retaining a ruthless reputation. So no matter how minor the offense, disrespect of any degree was inexcusable.

"A year from now, our lives will be much different than they are right now," Asha said as they were walking to the car. "And because failure isn't an option, and I truly believe we were born to be Queens, that means that we're only steps away from reaching the throne. And when we take our place, you better believe it's gon' people coming for us. And mark my words, most of 'em will be men who are too weak to stomach the success of independent women."

Noni nodded, allowing the wisdom and truth of her sister's words to fully resonate.

"The grittiest part of any construction is in the beginning," Asha continued, as they entered the car and reached for their seatbelts. "So we can't be afraid to get our hands dirty. Because if our shit ain't built right, or on a solid foundation, then the slightest breeze gon' blow us down."

"And our reputation is our foundation," Noni correctly asserted.

"Exactly!" Asha agreed. "So we gotta treat it and protect it for the precious thing it is. And we'll start with that clown you clashed with today. It needs to be known that you can't disrespect any member of the Mob and not suffer severe consequences. So once we do spread our wings, it'll be clearly understood that Butterfly Mafia is not to be taken lightly."

Noni bobbed her head in full agreement, then remembered to enlighten her sister on the existence of the Belle Isle recording.

"You gotta see it, love," Noni smiled at the recollection. "It's all over Facebook."

***

Later that night, the twins were idling in the parking lot of the club at which Lo-Lo danced. To prevent her from encountering any sort of dangerous situations, ranging from robbery to rape, they picked their girl up on whatever nights she worked.

As usual, Lo-Lo broke into a wide grin as she exited the club and saw the GTO. She loved the twins as if they were her biological sisters, and the sight of them waiting for her always warmed her heart with an indescribable feeling.

"There you go with cheesing shit," Noni teased as Lo-Lo crawled into the backseat.

Asha slammed the door shut and Noni sped off.

"Girl, you know I can't help it," Lo-Lo smiled, then leaned up front to kiss both of their cheeks.

"Did you have a good night?" Asha inquired over the growling pipes.

"I did alright," Lo-Lo shrugged. "I made close to eight hundred dollars, and I still got tomorrow."

While Asha didn't normally withhold information from Noni or Lo-Lo, if everything went according to plan, she had a secret surprise that would blow both their minds.

"So, what's this I hear about some niggas in there fucking with Lance?" Noni said as she weaved through traffic.

"Noni, you know you ain't got no gun license," Asha cut in before Lo-Lo could reply.

"And? What's that supposed to mean?"

"That means we can get pulled over if you don't slow this bitch down. Cherries and berries, as you like to say."

After a careful scan of her rearview and side mirror, Noni's foot bore further down on the gas.

"Fuck 'em!" she smiled, her diamond teeth twinkling like miniature stars. "Let 'em catch me if they can."

Shaking her head in amusement at her sister's reckless behavior, Asha settled back in her seat and enjoyed the ride.

Once they safely arrived at Lo-Lo's residence, Noni recalled her inquiry about Lance and turned in her seat. "Aye, you never did tell me what's going on with my lil buddy."

Relaying exactly what was told to her, Lo-Lo explained that Lance was basically being forced to pay for another's man mistake. "...So in the midst of him running from the guard, he threw some shit in my brother's shower. And since he left it in there and somebody else found it, they told him he gotta reimburse their loss."

"That's bullshit," Noni snarled, shaking her head in disgust. "Cause I would've did the same thing. Fuck I look like grabbing some shit and I don't even know what it is, or who it belongs to. But they picking a shot with Lance, cause they know don't nobody in there got his back. But what they don't know is that he got support out here, where it really matters at."

"I told him to get me their names and inmate numbers so I can look 'em up."

"Where he say these niggas from?" Asha chimed in.

"He thinks Flint."

"Aw, that ain't nowhere," Noni said, ready to take the trip tonight. "So soon as he shoot you that info, we gon' send them niggas a message that Lance Miller got the Mob in his corner."

After watching Lo-Lo enter the house, Noni double tapped the horn before driving off.

With the wheels of their minds turning as rapidly as the GTO's, the twins simultaneously glanced at each other; their eyes reflecting a humored feeling.

"What you over there thinking about?" Asha grinned, though she already knew the answer.

"Same thing as you," Noni grinned back.

"Tell me, love."

"I'm thinking we slide down on that nigga, Diesel, then go on a roundtrip to Flint. We send two messages with one envelope."

Her sister's tardiness, forgiven and forgotten, Asha beamed. "Long live the Mob!"

Chapter 8

Accompanied by Teer, all three members of the Mob were flying down the highway in a rented SUV. With Lo-Lo behind the wheel, they were en route to Ionia, Michigan.

Taking Teer's vouching at face value, along with the legendary tales attached to his cousin's name, the women were willing to welcome his family member into their fold. And while it was possible prison had dulled the blade of his morality, they were certain they'd detect a defective character. When you've journeyed through jungles since juvenile ages, you learned to spot a chameleon from a mile away.

Lo-Lo lowered the music as they turned into the parking lot of Ionia State Prison. Called I-Max for short, it was home to some of the most dangerous inmates in Michigan.

"I'll be right back," Teer said, reaching for the door handle, "I gotta let 'em know his ride here."

"Teer, ain't they gon' ask to see your ID?" Asha asked.

"Nah, cuz said just come in there and tell 'em his ride outside, and they gon' send for him."

As they watched Teer disappear inside the administration building, Noni wagered from the front seat. "I got twenty dollars that say he come back out with a light skin nigga that's sprayed and got long hair."

Asha shook her head, "Nah, Noni, I think you way off on this one. So I gotta foot massage against that twenty."

"Bet!" Noni called, reaching back to lock it in with a handshake.

Lo-Lo laughed at a sudden thought. "Noni, why you just sit here and describe a male version of yourself? Talking 'bout he gon' be light skin and tatted up. I'm surprised you ain't say he gon' have a diamond grill, too."

"I know, right!" Noni laughed, showcasing implants that had costed them a fortune.

Her laugh was short lived as Teer exited the prison, followed by a fellow only a few inches taller.

"Girl, you wasn't even close," Lo-Lo grinningly shook her head.

A darker version of Teer but minus the dreads, his cousin had a wild bush of hair and the youthful appearance of a mischievous teenager.

"Yeah, I'ma need you to make sure them rough ass hands nice and moisturized when we get home," Asha smiled before they stepped out the truck.

As Teer was introducing them to his cousin, who was known in the streets as Double-O, even Noni was initially discomforted by his soulless, dark eyes. At just 24 years of age, Double-O bore the stare of a stone cold killer.

With Noni encouraging Double-O to ride up front, the group piled inside the SUV and sped off.

"So, is that joint as raw as niggas say it is?" Noni inquired from the third row. "Or they just capping?"

"Let's just say a nigga ain't gotta go all the way to Afghanistan to be in no war," Double-O answered.

"But I'm saying, you on some super skinny shit," Noni bluntly commented. "So how the fuck was you able to keep them niggas off your ass?"

Already fond of her forward approach, Double-O smirked. "Because it ain't about the size of a nigga's height or his muscles."

"Then, what's it's about?" Lo-Lo curiously chimed in.

"The size of his heart and his knife."

There was a period of silence at the rawness of his response.

A mile later, Noni regrouped. "Aye, listen, we commend you for your acts of bravery, but that shit ain't rewarded with no stars and bars, you feel me. 'Cause the real war out here in these streets. And I don't know what all Teer done told you, but we about to get deep in these trenches and get it out the mud. And I hope you don't think just because we girls we can't get gritty. Because trust me, we can match the aggression of any nigga alive."

"I'm already hip," Double-O said, turning to lock eyes with Noni. "So, you ain't gotta convince me."

Noni frowned. "What you mean, you already hip?"

He smirked. "Just because a nigga locked up don't mean he ain't got access to the streets. You know how many times I done watched that Belle Isle video?"

At her surprised reaction, he replied, "The only thing we can't get in the joint is the key to the front door."

"But like I was saying," Double-O continued, as he turned back to stare straight ahead. "I'm already hip to the Mob. And they say you just as cold with the gloves as you is with a gun."

More amazed than shocked, the women couldn't believe their existence was known of and being spoken of inside a men's prison. They were nowhere near the height of their peak, yet they were being highly regarded in such a war like environment.

Over the course of their continued conversation, it was learned that Double-O had been a member of a renowned crew called The F.A.M. But after the death of his cofounding partner, and his own imprisonment, the crew ultimately came unglued.

"I think I remember hearing about that," Noni nodded. "Didn't one of them niggas kill their own brother, or some shit?"

"Nah, that's what everybody thought," Double-O corrected. "But come to find out, my nigga, King's girl was rocking us to sleep. And her sister was fucking with his brother, and they was turning them niggas against each other the whole time."

As Double-O recalled scenes from his past that were impossible to forget, he was also reminded of a promise he'd made King just days ago; that by all means would he resurrect his name and avenge his death.

Pushing the sides aside, Noni was ready to get to the meat of the matter. "Listen, it ain't no mystery we've heard the stories. And from what they say, you was out here on some James Bond type shit. But I'm saying, though, that was before you went and did a four-ball in I-Max. So my question to you is this. Nigga, is you shell shocked, or you ready to jump out and get them mu'fucking Chucks dirty?"

Double-O grinned as he turned to look toward the backseat. "I was told that words are beautiful, but actions are supreme. So in answer, I say pick a vic' and watch me work. Then, witness for yourself if my shit ain't superb."

Aside from the sinisterness of his smile, they noticed that his front tooth was indeed chipped.

***

Arriving back in Detroit, they took Double-O to the mall, at which time Teer slipped him a small bankroll as they exited the truck.

"It ain't much, cuz, but most of it is what the Mob put in. 'Cause I'm skinning fleas out here, you feel me."

"They gave you this for me?" he asked in mild disbelief, glancing back at the truck.

Teer nodded. "They ain't want to give it to you their selves, 'cause you know, they was taking a nigga's pride into consideration. I told you they was thorough like that."

"So, you really rocking with these girls, huh?"

Recalling how the twins embraced him when he was at his lowest, Teer replied, "Cuz, I was on some homeless shit out here when I met them. Nigga, I was robbing and stealing just to eat. But they took me in and took a chance on me. And believe me when I tell you, they don't be letting niggas in their circle like that. So for them to choose to rock with me, then hell yeah I'm rocking with them. And I'll die for either one of 'em without hesitation."

Deeply impressed by his cousin's allegiance, Double-O thoughtfully accompanied him into the mall.

No sooner than they passed through the front entrance, Lo-Lo turned in her seat. "Girl, you cut into that boy on some super aggressive shit. I was thinking to myself like, Lord, please don't let this man pull out no damn shank."

Noni shrugged. "There wasn't no sense in sugarcoating it. Because if he sensitive, we don't need him. And if he ain't ready to rock out, then we definitely don't need him. So, why waste time we can't get back?"

Lo-Lo looked to Asha for her outlook, to which she nodded in agreement. "I think Noni handled it accordingly. Because a man that was insecure or sensitive would've definitely got defensive. But by him keeping his composure, then we can assume he's someone that's sure of who he is. And that goes a long way, considering how emotional these niggas is out here. You'd think they were the ones bleeding every month."

They shared a chuckle at the truth before Asha continued, "But another thing, I had hollered at Teer the other day, just to get a feel for what we were walking into. And he basically said that his cousin caught it worse than him. He was the victim of child abuse. Then, he ran away when he was like twelve, and been in the streets ever since. So my point is, I think we might've gotten lucky with this one. Because I got a feeling Double-O is governed by the main quality we require."

"And what makes you think that?" Noni inquired, unable to predict the direction in which her sister was headed.

"Because if it's one thing I know, it's that the young males who've been deprived of love and affection at home are usually the ones who yearn to fill that void the most.

Especially, the ones who were born with loyal spirits. They be eager to lend out their loyalty, in hopes it'll be returned. How you think gangs initially became so popular? All them niggas ain't rough and tough. But most of 'em be looking for love and acceptance. And they'll do almost thing to get it, even if for some of them it means adopting a false image. But that just goes to show how strong that desire is. And I gotta feeling Double-O ain't no different. As long as we showing him genuine love, which someone of his nature can sense, then his loyalty will belong to us for as long as we're alive."

Lo-Lo and Noni wore contemplative looks at the conclusion of Asha's discourse. They were grateful to have a girl who could shed enlightenment on such a broad scale. And though the three were equal in age, it was uncontested that Asha was the Mob's mother figure.

Both bearing shopping bags in either hand, Double-O and Teer exited the mall nearly an hour later.

Immediately upon reentering the truck, Double-O expressed his gratitude toward the girls' generosity.

"Lil' cuz told me what y'all did," he said, offering eye contact to each of them, "And I just want to say I sincerely appreciate it. And not only on my behalf, but Teer's as well. Because y'all been looking out for him, something his own mama wouldn't do. So that alone says a lot in regards to who y'all are in character."

As Double-O paused and peered downwards, Asha could sense that he wasn't finished, but was searching for the right words to further express himself.

"Just speak from your heart," she earnestly encouraged him. "And we'll understand it, because that's the only language we know."

Double-O looked up, touched by the tenderness of Asha's tone. This was her first time speaking since they'd picked him up, so he had automatically assumed she was the meaner of the bunch. But from the gentle manner in which she had just addressed him, he knew his assumption was wrong. For Asha wasn't mean, but a watchful woman who was thoroughly cautious.

Freely speaking as he'd been instructed, Double-O spoke, "I've been in the trenches since I was eleven, and I've seen and heard about every form of betrayal and dishonesty there is. I know it's not often you cross paths with pure hearted people. So when or if you do, you gotta latch on to 'em and reciprocate that same energy. So, I'm saying, because of how y'all voluntarily embraced a 16-year-old boy, who wasn't even that old at the time, then there's no doubt in my mind that y'all honorable women. I stand by supreme actions. So until I'm shown otherwise, or my heart stop pumping, then I'ma give you the same level of loyalty as I would if you were my little sisters. And I pledge that on every moral and principle by which I stand."

Based on her instincts, with which she was intimately involved, Asha believed every syllable Double-O had spoken. For the truth held a unique ring, and she was fortunate to have been born with a distinctive ear.

"Double-O, I can't promise you we'll prevail," Asha truthfully admitted, "But I can promise you that whatever outcome awaits us, me and mines will be standing firm and faithful in the end. And I pledge that on all four wings of the Butterfly Mafia!"

Chapter 9

Wearing baggy shorts and a dingy tank top, Teer was dribbling a basketball through the Brewster projects. He was striving to display the handling skills of Allen Iverson but was looking more like a miniature Shaq.

When an attempted crossover sent the ball rolling towards a group of men who were loudly socializing behind a white van, Teer chased after it.

As he bent to scoop the Spaulding, a large Nike stepped on it in obstruction.

"You need to watch how you dribbling this dumb ass ball," growled a man's gravelly voice. "With your lil' dirty ass."

Looking upwards with a hurt disposition, Teer was staring into the scowling face of a felon named Diesel.

"I'm just trying to practice so I can make the team," Teer informed him in an innocent tone.

"Leave the lil homie alone, bruh," a man named Pierre spoke up. "He a fucking kid."

A lifelong resident of the streets, Pierre had seen his fair share of men who came home from prison with bully mentalities. And sad to say, majority of them had died violent deaths.

"You heard what I said," Diesel growled at Teer, reluctantly removing his foot. "Now, get your ball and scram, lil' nigga."

Teer was reaching down, when a hooded figure in all black appeared from one side of a nearby building and began advancing in their direction. With a hand shielded along its right leg, the gunman was firmly grasping a silver firearm.

A man standing beside Diesel happened to look to his left. Frozen in fear, his eyes widened at the sight of what appeared to be the Grim Reaper.

"Ohhh, shit!" Pierre exclaimed before he took off running.

Before Diesel could follow suit, the gunman raised the Taurus and put two in his torso. The remaining crowd scattered as Diesel collapsed with a sharp outcry.

Going to stand over him, the gunman ignored Diesel's pointless pleas and took careful aim. "This for Noni," the killer confessed before unflinchingly firing four rounds into his shaved crown.

With Diesel's destroyed head lying beside the ball that had been used as a distraction, the killer tossed the gun, then jogged to a car across the street and jumped into its passenger seat.

Disguised in a dark hoodie and sunglasses, Noni sped away from the curb as soon as the door shut.

She was halfway down the block, when Double-O snatched off his ski mask, eyes wild with excitement.

"That's how you put a nigga's head to bed!" he boasted, rocking in his seat to an imaginary beat.

Having witnessed the slaying through the front windshield, Noni encouragingly extended her hand for a pound.

"Yeah, you definitely hit dog with some shit. 'Cause I counted like six of them bitches!"

The ease with which he had murdered Diesel dissolved whatever doubts Noni may have harbored in regards to Double-O's reputation. It was clear that the four year absence had done little to lessen his love for violence. Impressed by an instinct she knew he naturally possessed, she could see herself and Double-O becoming best friends.

When she made a right turn at the next street and braked, Teer came running from in between two houses and dove into the backseat.

"Damn, cuz!" he proudly beamed as the car surged forward, "You wasn't fucking around."

60

Emphasizing each word with a movement of her head, Noni grinned in malicious triumph. "And that's how you send a muthafucking message!"

***

With Asha driving and Lo-Lo riding shotgun, the three culprits, who had changed clothing, were now reclining in the rear of the Suburban as it sped down the interstate. After leaving the thoroughly cleansed car parked in an alleyway, they were certain it was already being driven by an unsuspecting person, or people.

Guided by GPS as they arrived in Flint, Michigan, Asha was directed to what appeared to be the city's grittiest section.

"This shit look worse than Detroit," Noni commented, as they parked on a block lined with dilapidated houses and duplexes.

"And it's just as dangerous," Double-O inserted, recalling how a city so small had once been crowned the murder capital of America.

Along with sending his sister the full names and inmate numbers of his two oppressors, Lance had also included the torn piece of an envelope, which showed the address of a female in Flint. After waiting for the right time, Lance had snuck into one of the men's rooms during chow and rifled through his belongings until coming upon an old letter. And he knew from the man's obsession with talking that the female was the mother of his only child.

Forty minutes into their stakeout, a half-dead sedan turned down the block and parked in front of a light yellow Duplex.

Appearing to be in her mid-twenties, a bronze colored female exited the car. She wore a tired look as she opened the back door and reached in to remove a small child from its car seat.

"I'm coming with you," Noni said, as Asha was on the verge of emerging from the truck.

The woman was approaching the front porch of her building, when she glanced over her shoulder and saw the twins crossing the street. Not knowing what to think, as she took in the distinct difference in their appearances, she sat her child down and turned to confront them in a combative stance.

Asha raised her hands in a gesture of peace. "We ain't here for no trouble, love."

The woman didn't reply but continued to curiously peer between the two. Whereas Asha resembled a beige colored Barbie, Noni had the swagger of a successful rapper who was still knee deep in the streets.

"I'm Asha," she smiled, extending a hand that bore beautifully done nails with light blue butterflies. "And this my sister, Noni."

When the woman hesitantly shook her hand and introduced herself as D'Aura, Noni simply lifted her head in acknowledgment.

"So, what can I do for y'all? D'Aura inquired, as a cute little girl peeked from behind her leg.

Asha waved at the chubby child before answering, "I just need to talk to you about your peoples in Milan."

Scoffing at the thought of her child's father, D'Aura was on the verge of making a fly remark, when she had another, more concerning thought.

"How y'all know where I live?" she asked Asha with a suspicious squint. "Because Cody ignorant for sure, but not to the point where he'd give out my address."

"I understand you don't know us from a can of paint," Asha replied in a reasoning tone, "But this not a conversation we should have on your front porch. We're strangers, but not animals. And I'm not telling you to trust us, but I am telling you that you ain't got nothing to worry about."

Inside the small, threadbare apartment, Asha and Noni sat on a sunken couch. Though D'Aura kept the interior as tidy as possible, she was obviously struggling to make ends meet.

"So here's the thing," Asha began, as D'Aura took a seat across from them. "We gotta little buddy of ours in Milan that's like a younger brother. He gotta good heart, but not a tough bone in his body. But long story short, he was recently forced to pay for somebody else's fuck up, and your baby's father was the enforcer. I've been in that cage, so I know how people tend to torture the weak. But Lance is an exception. Because, other than a woman or child, it ain't nobody on earth we won't hurt on our little brother's behalf."

As D'Aura took in the speech with a thoughtful brow, her daughter ran up to her and whined, "Mama, I'm hungry."

"They didn't give you nothing to eat at daycare?"

The little girl lyingly shook her head.

"Alright, just give me a minute, and I'll see what we got."

Turning back to Asha, D'Aura said, "I hear what you saying, but what made y'all come to me?"

"We need you to deliver a message."

"And what's that?"

Asha leaned forward and handed D'Aura her phone. "Just scroll down."

There were pictures of people she immediately recognized. One was of an older man taking out the trash. Another of a teenage boy hanging out with his friends. And a few others, all of who were family members of her child's father.

D'Aura looked up from the phone in disturbance, to which Asha replied, "This not out first trip to Flint. Like I told you, we'll do everything in our power to protect our peoples. Even it means hurting someone else's. So, next time you talk to your child's father, help him understand that Lance Miller is off limits."

Asha and Noni rose from the couch.

"We appreciate your time," Asha said, reclaiming her phone. "And we meant no disrespect by coming by unannounced. I just figured by you and him sharing a child, he'd be more inclined to take your advice."

As D'Aura escorted them to the door, Asha asked Noni to wait for her in the truck.

Once the two were alone, Asha inquired about D'Aura's personal life. "From woman to woman, how bad are you struggling?"

D'Aura frowned at the boldness of her inquiry, to which Asha clarified, "Girl, ain't nobody judging you. Me and my twin been struggling all our lives. So don't let the nails and edges fool you. I'm only asking about your situation because I understand the struggle, and what it's like not to have help. Besides a man either wanting to get over on you or on top of you, then you really can't expect much else out of these new-age clowns. So shit, we all we got."

Bobbing her head in agreement, D'Aura smiled, "Yeah, you right about that."

"But, yeah, girl, we ain't doing much better," Asha admitted. "We just happen not to have kids. But whenever I cross paths with a woman who I can see potential in, it would be less of my character not to extend a hand. So tell me, how bad are you struggling?"

While it was difficult to verbally explain, there was something about a person's energy and demeanor that enabled you to instinctively detect that they were genuine in nature. You usually could just feel it. And this was an instance when D'Aura knew that Asha was unlike the average girl and was wise beyond her years.

D'Aura would go on to reveal how her child's father had went away without leaving anything of value behind. "I made a poor choice in who I chose to have a child with, but there ain't no sense in complaining now. I gotta figure it out. But to answer your question... I'm behind on rent, and my fridge ain't exactly full of food. I want to work a second job, but I can barely afford daycare as it is now. So I've been kind of stuck between a rock and a hard place."

D'Aura looked over her shoulder as the five-year-old was busily playing with her phone. "I love that little girl with every bone in my body. And it be eating at me when she ask for something and I have to say no, simply because I can't afford it. And she too young to understand that mommy ain't being mean, mommy just don't got it."

Although Asha couldn't relate, she could understand. And her heart went out to the woman and child. To the extent that she found herself digging into her pocket and removing every dollar she had.

"This only a few hundred," she said, holding it out to D'Aura. "So stretch this as far as you can. I got some moves in the works, and hopefully I'll be able to do more real soon."

With her mouth slightly parted in disbelief, D'Aura eyed the money before finally shaking her head. "Girl, I can't accept that. Because I don't have a clue when I'll be able to pay it back."

"Woman, if you don't stop being silly," Asha laughed, pressing the money into D'Aura's hand. "This ain't no loan. This just something to help you out until I can come back with more. I know you trying. I can tell by how clean you keep this place. Sometimes we just be needing a little push, that's all. So don't look at this as a gift from Asha but see it as a sign from the universe that's encouraging you to keep going."

After exchanging phone numbers and a big hug, Asha said she'd be in touch before turning to leave.

Closing the door after watching Asha descend the staircase, D'Aura gratefully looked down at the money, then over at her daughter. She then smiled to herself, thinking of how she would surprise the little girl with her favorite meal at McDonald's.

As soon as Asha reentered the truck, Noni was all over her. "What was you in there doing, twin?"

Filled with a euphoric feeling from her generous actions, Asha replied, "What real women do, love. Look out for each other."

As they drove back to Detroit, discussing an upcoming event that would decide the direction of their lives, neither of the three women could've known that they would soon encounter an unimaginable surprise.

Chapter 10

In a snug sweatsuit that showcased her curves, Asha was smelling good enough to eat as she knocked on the back door of a well- known weed house.

Moments later, the door was opened by a man big enough to be a lineman for the Lions. In the palm of his meaty left mitt was a chrome firearm.

"Damn, lil' mama," he lustfully grinned while stepping aside for her to enter. "What you doing out here alone at this time of night? Why you ain't got your man with you?"

"It's a shortage of real ones," she smiled back. "So I gotta fend for myself until one come along."

Scanning the yard before closing the door, the giant led her to a front room, where two men were on a couch, battling each other in a game of Madden.

As Asha was eyeing the items on a coffee table, which included an assault rifle, zip lock bags of various strands, and a digital scale, one of the men paused the game and looked up.

"What up doe?" he greeted with a steady gaze. If he was attracted to her cute features or curvaceous frame, there was no indication of it in his eyes.

"Yeah, let me get five grams," she answered, reaching into her pocket for the money.

"Don't I know you from somewhere?" the third man questioned.

Maintaining her composure, Asha calmly lied, "I done danced at almost every club in the city. So you might."

"Nah," he said, shaking his head, "I don't think that's where it's from."

"KP, your game weaker than shit, nigga," his friend teased as he dropped buds inside a baggie. "If you want her number, just ask for it. Most she can do is shoot you down."

As she was exchanging the money for the marijuana, KP pointed at her. "You from the Brewster's, ain't you?"

In spite of her galloping heartbeat, Asha shook her head, "Nah, boo, I ain't grow up in no projects. But like your friend said, all you had to do was ask."

Before he could continue his interrogation, Asha thanked them for their services and turned to leave.

"Bro, I think that's that bitch Noni's sister," Asha heard KP whisper as she was nearing the back door.

As intended, the death of Diesel had been awarded to Noni. It wasn't a coincidence he ended up dead shortly after their heated confrontation. But it was just Asha's luck that KP happened to be Diesel's younger brother.

While Asha didn't know who KP was, she did know she needed to exit that house. Inching her hand toward the small of her back, she was silently pleading for the giant to hurriedly unlock the door.

"What would you say if I was to ask for your number?" the giant smiled, his hand hovering over the lock.

"I'd say I gotta pee real bad, and I'll catch you next time."

Smirking at her rejection as he turned the lock, he had the door partially opened, when the sound of a chambering round came from in the front room.

"Aye, Dino, hold up!" KP yelled, as he hurried toward the kitchen.

With only a second to think, Asha drove a knee into the giant's groin. Then, as he doubled over in pain, she fled out the door.

When KP let off a few wild rounds and mindlessly chased after her, Double-O emerged from the darkness and tripped him. As KP tumbled to the ground, losing the rifle in the process, Double-O didn't hesitate to reunite him with his big brother.

The giant was raising his weapon in preparation to shoot, when Noni swiveled into the doorway and broke his nose with the butt of her gun. When he cried out before cupping his palm over the now crooked cartilage, she shot the hand in which he held the gun; forcing him to drop it.

Using his massive frame as a shield, Double-O and Noni guided the giant back inside the house.

"There was another one in the front room," Asha warned, as she trailed behind them with a weapon of her own.

"You better tell him to stand down," Double-O advised the giant, as they continued toward the living room. "Because you gon' be the first to get hit."

Yelling for his friend not to shoot, the giant urged him to just hand over the goods.

"Where KP at?" the friend inquired from behind the couch.

"He dead, nigga!" the giant shouted back. "Now give 'em that shit!"

Several silent seconds passed before the unarmed man slowly stood up.

"Y'all know who shit this is?" he bitterly cautioned, while removing money and Ziplock bags from inside the couch.

"Nah, whose is it?" Noni asked, though she already knew.

"This Big Dullah shit. And he definitely gon' find out who –"

Before he could complete the statement, Double-O swung his semi toward the staircase and let off five rapid shots.

The twins stared in awe as a half-naked dead man and his gun came tumbling down the steps. Thankful to have a Double-O on their team, there was no denying the validity of the man's valor.

Noni withdrew a trash bag from inside her pants leg and tossed it to Asha.

Wedging her weapon in her waistband, Asha quickly scooped their spoils into the bag and slung it over her shoulder.

At pointblank range, Double-O fired a round into the giant's right temple.

As he toppled over in what seemed like slow motion, the last man standing made a run for the front door.

In the calmest manner, Noni sighted her semi with his spine and fired twice.

When he slid down the door, leaving a blood streak along the way, Double-O attentively watched as Noni went to stand over him.

"Tell Dullah I said fuck him when you see him," she coldly spat before spilling his brains onto the carpet.

She might be rawer than Puma, Double-O thought to himself, as he recalled another female he knew who'd also been vicious. The trio were on the verge of leaving, when Asha saw something that made an informative light turn on in her head.

"Aye, y'all hold up," she said, pausing to thoughtfully stare at the man who tumbled down the steps.

When they turned to eye her with curious stares, her following statement surprised them both. "It's somebody else in here."

Noni frowned, reflexively tightening her grip on the gun. "Why you say that?"

"This nigga practically in his draws. And you don't get undressed in no trap house and go to sleep. This nigga was up there fucking."

Their eyes were simultaneously drawn to the top of the darkened staircase. To avoid a full scale war with Dullah, it was of utter importance that they leave behind no witnesses... even if it meant murdering a woman.

Creeping up the staircase with the stealth of Rangers, they split into two groups at the top and went in search of their prey.

As Asha and Noni checked the bathroom, Double-O nudged open a bedroom door with the toe of his shoe.

Clutching his weapon in both hands as he entered the room in a slightly crouched position, he first took in the mattress on the floor and the pile of clothes beside it. From there his gaze went over to the closed door of a closet, which was the only place for a person to hide.

Double-O went into a full crouch as he edged toward the closet. If there was an armed person inside, they'd likely shoot upwards upon the door being opened.

Slowly turning the knob, he swung the door open and braced himself for an eruption of gunfire.

When nothing happened after nearly a minute, he drew a deep breath before turning into the doorway.

Also crouched down, a dark skin girl returned his stare from a corner of the small enclosure. With her crossed arms covering her naked breasts, her plump figure was shivering from the freezing temperature of fear.

Double-O rose to his full height and aligned his weapon with her wig. While he found no pleasure in taking a woman's life, he'd been given specific instructions to leave no one alive.

As the girl closed her eyes and awaited the bullet that would free her from a life of pain and suffering, the twins entered the room and curiously approached the closet.

At the same time that Double-O pulled the trigger, Asha yelled, "Wait!" and shoved his hand.

Narrowly missing the intended target, the bullet entered the wall just centimeters from the girl's head.

Pushing Double-O aside, Asha squatted down so that her and the girl were eye level.

"Shawna," she called in affection, reaching out to lay a tender hand on the girl's knee.

When her eyes reluctantly blinked open, she gasped in shock before covering her mouth. As if seeing a ghost, she couldn't believe the image that was presently before her. Then, as reality settled in, she shamefully lowered her head and quietly wept. For her closest and only friends would disappointingly learn that she had fell weak and returned to the comforting arms of her drug addiction.

As Asha laid her gun on the floor and consolingly took Shawna in her arms, Noni bent down to join in on the hug. She loved and cared for the girl just as much.

Double-O couldn't believe his eyes. They had just committed a quadruple murder, and his two accomplices were hugged-up and crying at the crime scene.

"Aye, listen, I hate to break up y'all reunion, or whatever," he finally interrupted, "But this ain't exactly the time or place to be having it. We gotta get the fuck out of here."

Regaining her composure, Asha wiped her eyes and instructed him to grab Shawna's clothes. She'd been so overwhelmed with emotion, that she had temporarily forgotten where they were.

After fleeing out the back door, they crossed an alleyway and went in between two abandoned houses. First checking to ensure the coast was clear, they ran across the street to the Suburban, where Lo-Lo and Teer sat up front.

As they piled inside the SUV, Lo-Lo rose up in her seat and brought the engine to life. "I was starting to get worried about y'all. We heard all the shoo—"

Lo-Lo's words trailed off as she turned to look in the backseat.

"Shawna!" she exclaimed, her eyes bulging in disbelief. "Oh my God, girl!"

Growing frustrated at the girls' lack of concern towards being caught, Double-O leaned in Lo-Lo's line of vision.

"Unless y'all wanna continue this reunion in the county, then I suggest you put this bitch in drive."

As the SUV slid through the city's darkened streets, Asha held Shawna in her arms, whispering words of encouragement while rubbing the girl's hair.

"I'm sorry, Asha," Shawna softly apologized.

"For what, love?"

"For falling weak and getting back on that stuff again. But I was just so lost without y'all, and I didn't know what to do. I thought I would never see you again."

Without the funds to feed her heroin addiction, Shawna had recently succumbed to the soliciting of her 18-year-old body. She would feel shameful after each encounter, but she needed the drugs to help numb the pain. Besides taking her life, there was no other way to escape the miserable conditions of what she considered a worthless existence.

Asha kissed Shawna on the forehead. "Do you remember what I told you when we last saw each other?"

Shawna nodded, recalling a promise she had thought of on a daily basis.

"I told you I'd find you, and that's exactly what I did. And it doesn't matter how or where it happened, or what condition you're in. All that matters is the four of us are back together. And this time, there'll be no separation."

Unbeknownst to Teer or Double-O, the girl, Shawna, was officially the fourth wing of the Butterfly Mafia.

Chapter 11

Smoking a Black-N-Mild cigar, an average height, light skinned man was leaning against a Silverado, when a pearl-white Mercedes Benz truck turned down his block.

The sparkling G63 braked beside him and the passenger window lowered midway. With her slanted eyes hidden behind oversized shades, Unique nudged her head for him to hop in back.

He pulled on the cigar before flicking it, then blew a cloud of smoke upwards and stepped up into the truck.

"What's good, Queen?" he greeted Mecca, settling beside her on tan interior. He took in a fast food bag on the seat between them but thought nothing of it.

Wearing dark clothing and an equally grim frown, she spoke without turning as the truck rolled forward. "I need your help, Smurf."

"Anything," he hastily replied, recalling the blessing she had once bestowed.

"I need you to find out who put that play down at Belle Isle a few weeks ago."

Smurf inwardly cringed at the weight of her request. "I'll do everything I can," he assured her in a halfhearted tone, "But I'ma tell you right now, it's a possibility I won't be able to come through. I mean, the video of it all over Facebook, but niggas ain't talking. I ain't heard a name mentioned yet. And that's unheard of 'cause you know how the streets talk."

Mecca nodded, knowing exactly what he meant. She too had eyes and ears all over the city, yet no one had a clue as to who was responsible. But she knew from the footage that they were dealing with an untamed animal. An animal she was desperate to put down.

"So, how you been living?" Mecca genuinely inquired, as her male driver aimlessly drove through the city.

Smurf flashed a subtle smile. "Shit, thanks to you, I got the game in a mean headlock. And these paws ain't touching nothing but the paper, you hear me.

It was indeed because of Mecca that Smurf was able to surpass majority his peers in the drug game. Because several years ago, she had dumped a large quantity of fentanyl and heroin his lap, with instructions to simply give her half the proceeds. A skilled chemist, Smurf had bubbled beyond belief. And it was for that reason he felt obligated to fulfill her current request.

"I gotta somebody I'ma holler at," he informed Mecca, as her driver turned back onto his street. "I be looking out for this lil nigga from the Brewsters, and they say it ain't nothing he don't know something about. So hopefully he done heard something that we ain't. And if so, I'ma definitely tune you in."

Expressing her gratitude towards his willingness to help, Mecca encouraged him to stay safe and alert. "And if you hear anything, hit my line at whatever hour."

As Smurf was exiting the truck, Mecca called out, "Aye, you forgot something."

When he turned to look back at her, she pointed at the fast food bag on the seat. "Take that with you."

"What is it?" he asked, curiously bending to grab it.

"Cheese. So let it be known that you willing to pay fifty grand for the name of the shooter. And I'm trusting you to use your judgement and filter out the real from the fuckery. But understand, the money is simply for the name, and nothing more. This was against family, so it's up to family to see to it that revenge is properly served."

Fully aware of the treacherous manner in which Mecca and Unique operated, Smurf could only imagine what tactics they'd use on whoever was responsible. But for a free fifty grand, he'd utilize every resource he had in uncovering the shooter's identity.

As the Benz pulled off, Smurf put the money in his Silverado and made a phone call. His investigation had officially begun.

"Hello?" answered the person on the other end.

"Pierre, what's good, my baby?" Smurf cheerfully greeted. "Where you at, bro? I need to link up with you. I'm trying to put a few dollars in your pocket."

***

As Noni was on the floor doing her morning exercise, which consisted of push-ups, sit-ups, and 200 squats, Asha was lying across the bed feeling perplexed. They were elated by their reunion with Shawna, but frustrated at the fact that they were forced to start over in their pursuit of prosperity.

Because Shawna suffered from a heroin addiction for the second time, they decided to seek professional help and admitted her into a drug rehab, where she'd spend the next six months. Choosing a facility with excellent reviews and a host of success stories, its fee amounted to pretty much every pound and penny they pillaged from the robbery. Luckily, Teer and Double-O had been understanding, as they'd basically been fed scraps for their services.

The twins had considered robbing another one of Dullah's drug houses but knew he would've beefed up security by now. There would be more men and bigger guns. So that move was clearly out of the picture.

"So, what's the plan, love?" Noni asked, as she completed a set of military-style push-ups.

Before Asha could answer, her phone buzzed on the bed from an incoming text. Reaching to grab it, she scoffed at the summons from Dullah.

"What?" Noni nosily inquired, pausing in midst of a sit-up.

Asha showed her the screen, to which Noni read and laughed. "He want to ask us about that robbery."

"Robbery?" Asha frowned in alleged confusion. "What robbery?"

Smirking in amusement, Noni rose up and replied, "Aw, you ain't heard? One of his weed spots got robbed the other day. And like four of his men got boxed."

Asha lifted her eyebrows in surprise. "Whaaaat?"

"Mmm, hmm," Noni giggled.

"Well, we better go see this what this clown want," Asha said, moving to get out of bed. "Before he get to thinking we had something to do with it."

Not knowing what to expect, the twins equipped themselves with right-sided shoulder holsters. Securing Glock 22's inside its case, the lefties threw on matching Moncler jackets.

After Asha peeked out of a downstairs window for suspicious pedestrians or peculiar cars, they marched outside to the GTO.

"I'm telling you right now, twin," Noni said while bringing the 454 crate engine to life. "If this nigga utter any disrespect out his bitch ass lips, I'ma clap him where he stand."

Although Asha understood her sister's frustration, especially after the latest stunt Dullah pulled in relation to the payment shortage, she also knew that now was not the time to be governed by emotion. The man was supported by a sizable army, so it would be suicidal to launch an attack right now. They lacked the finances and firearms, which were two key necessities when it came to winning wars.

"Let me see your gun, Noni," Asha said, extending her hand.

Noni snatched her eyes off the road and cried, "For what!"

"Because we not about to roll up in there on no cowboy shit. I don't mind you killing him, but not at the expense of our lives. Girl, we own a few handguns. We'd be dead in a day if we waged war with these niggas right now."

Noni bore a contemplative look as she steered through traffic with her left hand.

"Yeah, you right," she soon conceded, nodding her head. "So can I keep my gun?"

Smiling in warmth at her sister, Asha reached over to lay a hand on her shoulder. "You can keep your gun, Noni. And I'm not telling you not to use it, I'm just saying let's play it by ear first. And if shit don't feel right, we'll stand over this nigga together."

As Noni turned into the scrapyard, she passed by a self-drive Tesla. Locking eyes with its dark complected driver, she had no way of knowing she was staring at Unique.

Pulling up to the garage, its door began to raise before Noni could stick her head out. Once it was fully uplifted, her and Asha stared in surprise at what awaited them inside.

Along with a scowling Dullah, six of his soldiers stood on either side of him, shouldering high powered assault rifles.

"This a scare tactic," Asha said as Noni coasted inside. "Like any dog, he only gon' bite if we show fear."

Interlocking their hands as a gesture of strength and support, the twins exchanged a brief glance before boldly exiting the car.

"What type of greeting is this, Dullah?" Asha inquired, as her Noni planted themselves in front of GTO's grill.

Without responding, Dullah walked within inches of Asha and peered deeply into her unblinking eyes.

"Somebody robbed one of my spots," he finally spoke, after failing to detect a scent of fear or unease.

"That's unfortunate," Asha replied with direct eye contact. "But you still haven't answered my question. Because clearly it don't require all this to tell me your spot got hit."

Intensely eyeing her a moment longer, he held up a hand and his henchman obediently lowered their weapons.

Dullah cut his eyes at Noni, who was already watching him like a hawk. He smirked before returning his attention to Asha. "Why does your sister harbor so much hatred towards me?"

"I wouldn't call it hatred," Asha lied, "It's more like disappointment."

"Disappointment?"

"Dullah we've been loyal to you since we became your employees. We had never spoken one ill word against you, not even in private. So, naturally we was disappointed when you downplayed our desire for growth. We didn't ask to cut ties, we just asked for bigger roles. But you not only denied us, you had Rome short change us for a mistake we didn't even make."

"I had nothing to do with that," he lied with a straight face. "And I already chastised him for it, so you don't gotta worry about it ever happening again. And far as giving y'all bigger roles, look at what just happened to four of my men. That could've easily been y'all two, had I complied with your wishes. So you should be seeing my denial as a blessing."

Asha smirked. "If you say so, Dullah."

Noni stepped forward to address her sister, "What's up, twin, you ready to bounce? 'Cause this nigga giving me an ear infection."

Asha grinned, in spite of herself. Noni was something else. She bit her tongue for no one, which Asha knew could one day prove harmful. She just prayed she was always around to watch over her.

"Noni, you always got some fly shit to say to me," Dullah gritted with a vicious glare.

"If you don't like it, make my mouth bleed, Dullah."

He scoffed, "You really think you're a man, don't you?"

She scoffed right back, "And you really think you're one, don't you?"

Dullah clenched his fists and Noni stepped back to assume a fighter's stance.

"That big shit don't read with me, nigga. You gon' have to show me you got work."

As Asha quickly inserted herself between them before a punch could be thrown, two of Dullah's men came to stand alongside him. The hostility of their gaze sent a clear warning: it wouldn't be a fair fight.

"Noni, you making me think you might've had something to do with that shit!" Dullah aimed an accusing finger at her.

"And you making me wish I had!" she shouted over Asha's shoulder.

"I don't give a fuck if I gotta spend a fortune, I'ma find out what happened," Dullah solemnly promised.

"And let me be the first to know when you do," Noni retorted, as Asha ushered her back into the car.

Closing the passenger door, Asha went to confront Dullah before joining her sister. "If you think she involved, then that means you accusing me, too. Because my twin don't do shit without me knowing about it. And you know that. So, is that where we stand, Dullah?"

His chest heaving in anger, he averted his eyes. "Right now, I don't know where we stand. But I do know that from now on, if you can't come alone, then don't come at all. Because I've had enough of your sister's disrespectful ass mouth. I've killed for way less."

Asha forced herself not to heatedly respond to the latter part of his statement. "Alright, give me a call when you calm down, Dullah. I know you got a lot going on at the moment, but I'm hoping we can come to some sort of understanding."

Slipping a slight nod to Dullah and his demons, Asha went around to the driver side of the GTO and hopped in.

As she reversed out the garage, then whipped the car around and kicked up rocks, one of the men beside Dullah spoke, "What's the word, big homie? Because I'll murder both them bitches by midnight." He turned his evil eyes toward Dullah and added, "Free of charge."

Chapter 12

Entering the visiting area of the rehab facility, Shawna lit up like a kid on Christmas at the sight of her three best friends. Before their unexpected reunion, it had been over three years since she'd last saw them.

"Hey, y'all!" she greeted in excitement, giving each girl a long bear hug and a kiss on the cheek.

"Look at you," Lo-Lo smiled, holding Shawna at arm's length. "You already starting to resemble your old self."

As they settled around a round table, Asha grasped one of Shawna's hands and inquired, "So how is it, so far?"

"It's good, actually. They really pay attention to you, and the living conditions are about as nice as I assume it can get. And everybody has their own counselor. I mean, mine can't really relate, but she's very understanding."

Noni reached out to run a hand through Shawna's thick grade of hair. "Girl, one of the first places we taking you when you get out is to a beauty salon. They gon' have fun playing with all this damn hair."

Asha smiled at Shawna in affection, squeezing her hand. "We missed you so much. There wasn't a day that went by when we didn't think of you. And we just want you to know that you'll never be alone again. We're here for you, love, as we've always been."

Shawna began to tear up, and Noni playfully scolded her. "Girl, you better not start that in front of all these people. They gon' think we crazy if they look over here and see four crying women."

Through their laughter, Shawna picked up on a troubling look in Asha's eyes. She may have been a bit naive and not as emotionally sturdy as she'd like, but she was in tune with her instincts. And right now her intuition informed her something was wrong with her friend.

As their laughter subsided into a lapse of silence, Shawna inquired of Asha, "What's wrong, love?"

She looked up to meet Shawna's searching gaze, not sure of how to respond. The girl was going through enough as it was, and Asha didn't want to burden her with problems beyond her control.

"Don't worry, it's nothing," Asha replied with a subtle shake of her head. "We just need you to focus on getting better, so we can get you to the nearest tattoo shop."

Shawna was quiet for a minute, before instinctively asking, "How much did it cost to get me in this place?"

Their collective reaction to her question enabled Shawna to identify the source of their problem. Her friends had spent their entire savings on saving her. Touched so deeply by a sacrifice that solidified their love and loyalty, it was in that moment when Shawna knew with certainty that these were the three girls with whom she'd stand until the depletion of her oxygen supply.

Leaning forward, Shawna flashed a mischievous smile before announcing in a secretive tone, "I think I gotta enough money to cover whatever y'all spent."

They frowned in confusion at her statement. Because surely she didn't have the amount they had shelled out for her six month stay.

"Shawna, this shit ain't run us a few pennies," Noni blatantly admitted. "Girl, we talking about five figures."

She nodded. "I got that."

Despite the doubtful looks on Lo-Lo and Noni's faces, Asha sensed the truthfulness in her revelation and leaned forward. "Shawna, exactly how much money are you talking about?"

She hesitated for dramatic purposes, then answered with emphasis, "Fifty thousand."

"Fifty thousand?" Noni blurted, then quickly covered her mouth at the attention drawn by her sudden outburst.

Grinning broadly, Shawna said, "Remember my girl, Puma, I told y'all about?"

They bobbed their heads in unison, recalling the stories from her, as well as the others that still circulated throughout the city. In fact, Noni had been compared to Puma on a number of occasions. It was once jokingly stated that she may have been the reincarnated version of her.

"Well, one day we was out in the woods," Shawna continued, "And she was teaching me how to shoot a gun. You know, as a way of protecting myself. Anyways, once we was done, she had me stand in a certain spot while she went to the car and got a shovel. Then, she dug a hole and put the money in it. She said that if anything ever happened to her, I'd have something to fall back on."

Impressed by Puma's foresight, and even more so by her profound love for Shawna, the three girls developed an even deeper respect for someone they wish they could've had the privilege of meeting.

"Shawna, how long ago was this?" Lo-Lo asked.

"Like four years."

They groaned in discouragement, as it was likely the location was no longer accessible. For all they knew, the money was buried beneath a shopping mall by now.

"Why didn't you ever go get it?" Noni asked with a puzzled look, thinking of Shawna's prior predicament. Though they'd never bring it up, the girl had been bartering her body for drugs.

"Puma died when I was fourteen, and I was scared to bring that much money to my granny house. If her or my uncle would've found it, they would've took all of it. So I didn't know what to do but leave it where it was."

Shawna lowered her head before quietly continuing, "Then, once I got hooked on that stuff, there was no way I could spend Puma's money like that. Because I felt like that would've been me betraying her. So I chose to degrade myself, rather than betray the only person who had ever shown me love."

Asha scooted her chair closer and placed a comforting hand around Shawna. "Your loyalty is uncommon, love. Because the average addict would've blew through that all that money. So I'm sure that even though you fell weak, your moral discipline put a smile on Puma's face. And whether you realize it or not, you actually proved just how strong you really are."

Shawna looked up, and Asha nodded in confirmation. "That was raw will power. And everybody ain't got that."

Shawna allowed herself a subtle smile as she had never thought about it like that. And she recalled how Puma used to always confirm her inner strength. So maybe it was time she started believing in herself as much as others did.

"Shawna, I love you to death, girl, and you know that," Noni said in a serious tone, "But we need to go dig up that paper!"

Her bluntness brightened the mood, as the four women shared a round of laughter.

"Noni, why you always gotta be so silly?" Lo-Lo pushed her. "We was just having a sentimental moment."

"Girl, we really gon' be sentimental when we counting up fifty racks," she factually replied. "Because Lord knows we ain't never seen that much money before."

Shawna looked to Asha for direction. "What you want to do?"

She blinked in deep thought several times, then asked, "Do you remember exactly where it is, or you gotta look for it?"

"No, I remember. I walk five steps back from the tree and turn."

"Alright, we'll come back later tonight and sneak you out. But we gotta have you back before sunrise."

At the conclusion of their visit, they again gave Shawna bear hugs and cheek kisses.

"Remember," Asha said, "We'll be parked outside at twelve thirty. And fix your bed to where it look like somebody in it. Just in case they do a round before you come back."

Giving Shawna another hug and quick kiss, Asha led Lo-Lo and Noni out of the visiting room, turning in the doorway to wave as Shawna longingly stared after them.

As they were signing out, Asha saw something that made her tap Noni on the sly.

When Noni looked at her, Asha nudged her head toward the female receptionist. With an olive complexion and long, silky strands of dark hair, she was pretty enough to be the centerfold in Playboy.

Before Noni could question what her sister was implying, the woman looked up and locked eyes with her. Although the exchange was brief, it was wired with enough electricity to shock Noni into action.

Approaching the counter with a self-assured swagger, she offered her hand and a sparkling smile. "I'm Noni."

The receptionist revealed even white teeth as she softly took Noni's hand in her own. "I'm Angel."

Noni looked down and chuckled to herself.

"What?" Angel curiously inquired.

Gazing into the windows of Angel's soul, Noni answered, "I'm the devil, love. You gorgeous, but it would be wrong of me to corrupt an Angel."

Noni tapped the counter in farewell. "Blessings."

"Wait," Angel called, as Noni spun to leave.

When she turned back, Angel flirtatiously stated, "Wasn't the devil originally an Angel? So don't let the

86

features fool you. Because who's to say I haven't already been corrupted."

Noni withdrew her iPhone and held it out. "Call your phone."

Saving Angel's number under Heaven, Noni promised to reach out later and left the girl bubbling with a belly full of butterflies.

"That was fast," Lo-Lo said as they were exiting the facility. "What did you tell her?"

"What works every time..." Noni smiled. "The truth!"

***

It was 12:32 a.m., when Shawna came scuttling from on side of the facility. Having squeezed through her room's window, she had carefully constructed her bed to appear as if she was sound asleep beneath the comforter.

Shawna hopped in the passenger seat and Asha pulled off before she could fully close the door. The money was important, but so was Shawna's recovery; the reason for which Asha wanted to return her to the rehab as soon as possible.

As they rode in silence, Shawna took in Asha's dark attire, then glanced in the backseat at Lo-Lo and Noni and suddenly exploded in laughter.

"What's so funny?" Asha smiled.

"Nah, it's just –" Shawna started laughing again. "It's just, they sitting back there, looking all serious and stuff, with them big ass metal shovels laying across their laps. Like they ready to do some serious digging."

As the image caused them all to erupt in laughter, Shawna increased its volume by adding, "I forgot to tell y'all that she only buried it a few feet deep."

Turning down a dark one way street, Asha drove to the end of the block, looped the car around and parked.

After scanning the area for nosy neighbors, she killed the engine and they exited the car, bringing along only one shovel.

Shawna guided them through a field that led to the wooded area.

Clicking on a flashlight as they entered the forested area, she followed the same path Puma had taken four years ago.

"This some creepy shit," Noni whispered, her head swiveling nonstop.

As they came upon what Shawna believed to be the burial site, she slowly shined the flashlight in search of a certain tree.

After several minutes of her being unable to locate it, Asha asked her what she was looking for.

"It was a tree with a hole at the bottom of it. I told her it looked like something squirrels would live in. But I don't see it. I think it's too dark. We gotta come back in the day-time."

***

Later that morning, Noni strode into the rehab facility and walked up to the front counter, where Angel held up a finger as she was on a phone call.

"Well, well, well," she said upon disconnecting the call, "I assume you showed up to apologize in person for not calling me last night."

"I don't recall given you a specific time when I'd call. But if you wanted me to, then you can't fault me for not being a mind reader."

Stung by her sharp reply, Angel was thinking of an even sharper response, when Noni leaned over the counter. "I need a serious favor."

"Hold up, wait a minute," Angel said, forming a timeout sign with her hands. "First, you come up in here on some smart mouth ass shit, now you talking about a favor? Are you being for real right now?"

"I'm as solid as they're made," Noni stamped with conviction. "So don't let something so trivial prevent you from finding out."

After a deliberating pause, Angel sighed in submission, "What kind of favor are you talking about?"

"I just need to borrow my girl, Shawna Perry, for like forty minutes to an hour."

"You know a walk off is an automatic termination of her contract, don't you?"

"Listen to me, we gave up damn near every dollar we had to get her in here. So if this wasn't extremely important, this conversation would've even be taking place right now."

Angel held her gaze for a moment before finally voicing her consent, "Alright. But you better have her back here in exactly one hour, and not a minute later."

Noni touched her heart in gratitude. "I owe you big."

"You damn right, you do," Angel suggestively smiled.

Escorting Shawna out the facility's front door, Noni winked at her sister in triumph as they were approaching the car.

"It's only two things I've never seen in my whole life," Noni jokingly stated, as the car took off with a loud screech.

"And what's that?" Lo-Lo smiled, already knowing the answer.

"A UFO... and a hoe that won't go!"

When they returned to the wooded area, they discouragingly learned that the tree was no longer there. Shawna was able to pinpoint the spot her in which her and Puma had stood while target practicing, but that was the only clue given.

Closing her eyes, Shawna envisioned one of the last afternoons her and Puma had spent together. She saw Puma standing behind her, instructing her to stare through the semi's sights for accuracy. She saw Puma picking up the spent shell casings and placing them inside her backpack.

Shawna opened her eyes but continued to relive that afternoon.

Witnessing the dreamy look in her eyes, Asha and the others stepped aside to watch in fascination as Shawna began retracing four-year-old footsteps.

Shawna saw Puma point at the tree and ask what was noticeable about it. She saw herself staring at the hole in its base and making the comment about the squirrels. She recalled Puma telling her to stand directly in front of the tree, then walk five steps backwards and turn.

She looked down at the ground on which she stood, then back up at Noni, who held the shovel. "Dig right here in front of my feet."

Driving the shovel into the hardened soil, Noni began earnestly digging.

Other than the sounds of dirt being scooped and tossed, there was a suspenseful silence among the four women.

Several feet into the earth, Noni felt the shovel's blade come into contact with a solid object. She threw the shovel aside and resumed digging with her bare hands.

As the others edged closer with quickening heartbeats, Noni removed a brick shaped package from the earth.

"Give me something to open it with!" she barked, wiggling her fingers in impatience.

Asha tossed her the car keys, which she used to carefully cut into the thoroughly wrapped package.

Their eyes grew wide as saucers as she unveiled several mounds of money enclosed in saran. Had they not already known the exact amount, they would've sworn they were eyeing at least $100,000.

Drunk off euphoria, Noni fell flat on her back and screamed, flailing her arms and legs in a joyful tantrum.

As Lo-Lo and Asha joined in on the jubilation, Shawna rolled her eyes toward the Heavens and offered Puma a silent word of gratitude.

Thank you so much, sister. For everything. You were the first person to show me what love felt like, and you'll be my final thought on whatever day I'm called to join you. From bottom of my soul, I love you, girl.

Chapter 13

With Double-O riding shotgun, Asha turned into the parking lot of a Baptist Church. Pulling around back, she cut the wheel wide, threw the car in reverse and placed its rear end to the building.

She noticed a subtle smirk on his face. "What's all that?"

He shook his head, "Nah, it's just how you backed this bitch in without even being told. Some shit come from experience; you feel me. So I was just admiring your gangsta, that's all."

Despite her being younger in age, Double-O had to admit that Asha was definitely on point. She bore the exceptional character of a young lady who was destined to deliver empowerment.

Exiting the car in clothing suitable for Sunday service, the pair marched around to the front of the church, where Double-O grasped the door handle and froze.

Behind him, Asha frowned, "What's up?"

He turned to face her with a furrowed brow. "I ain't never been in no church before. So I wonder what this shit 'bout to feel like?"

"I couldn't tell you," Asha shrugged, "Because I ain't never been in one myself. But it's only one way to find out."

Double-O held the door open in courtesy and she breezed into the building like a devout Baptist.

Service was over, but a few attendants were still conversing in the pews, as several children laughingly ran around.

As Double-O considered which direction to take, his searching glare was observed by an elderly woman, who approached them with a warm smile. "How may I help you two lovely young people?"

"Yes, ma'am, I'm here to see Reverend Daniels."

"Oh, that's my son," she proudly beamed. "If you follow me, I'll take you to his office."

During the short excursion, Double-O kept his eyes focused on the floor, while Asha curiously took in her surroundings. And to her surprise, she didn't feel as uncomfortable as she had initially assumed she would.

"You know I'm not a bad person, God," she found herself silently praying. "I'm just working with what I know."

Knocking before entering, the elderly woman opened the door and stuck her head in. "Son, there's a young man and woman here to see you."

Settled behind a massive desk, Reverend Daniels laid down a pen and motioned for her to bring them in.

As Double-O and Asha entered the room, the Reverend rose to greet them with firm handshakes. "How are God's children?"

"We good, Rev, how you?" Double-O responded.

"Blessed by the best, so I can't complain."

Standing at 6'3", the forty-three-old Reverend was wiry built with salt and pepper hair. And though he was a man of the cloth, the hardness of his stare belied his humble demeanor. For the cloak wearing Reverend had once been a notorious gangster, widely known throughout the streets as Freddie-D.

"Have a seat," Reverend Daniels gestured before having one himself. "Now tell me, how can I help you?"

Double-O leaned forward and explained, "I didn't want to say it over the phone, but I'ma close friend of Kavoni's. And he said you could help me if I ever needed it. And I wouldn't be here if I didn't."

"But Kavoni has been dead for over two years," the Reverend replied, "So, why are you just now showing up?"

Double-O smirked. "Sir, I just left Kavoni at I-Max a month ago."

"Is that so?"

Double-O nodded. "We lived on the same range."

Reverend Daniels removed a prepaid phone from his desk drawer and tossed it to Double-O. "Well, if what you're saying is true, then get him on the phone."

Without delay, Double-O punched in a number and put the phone on speaker.

After a series of rings, the call was answered by a silent greeting.

"This Double-O, my baby."

"Aw, what up, bro?" Kavoni now spoke. "I was wondering when you was gon' call."

"Yeah, I jumped straight back on the field, you feel me. So shit been lightweight moving super-fast, bro. But check it out, I'm sitting here with your peoples right now, Reverend Daniels."

"What's good with the big homie? Kavoni cheerfully addressed him.

"I'm well, little brother, and you?"

"Maintaining, my baby, maintaining. And I apologize for not reaching out in a while, but sometimes a man don't be in a talkative mood. You know how it is, Rev."

"Indeed I do. So I'm assuming this man is a friend of yours."

"He is. And worthy of being yours, too."

Reverend Daniels trusted Kavoni's word like it was decreed by the Most High himself. Because not only was he upstanding in character, but he had once proven his loyalty on a grand scale.

"Aye, listen, y'all, I gotta go," Kavoni said in a lowered tone. "It's about to be count time and I gotta put this phone up. But Double-O, you stay alert out there, and keep in touch. So, hopefully we can bring some closure to that one demo. And Rev, forgive me for my selfish and inconsiderate behavior. You a true friend. And if you can, help my lil mans with whatever it is he's asking. And I'll be in touch soon. Luh y'all."

Once the call was disconnected, Asha was still reeling in disbelief. To have heard the voice of a villain viewed as one of the most vicious the city had ever bred was an experience she wouldn't soon forget.

Regarding Double-O with a more friendly smile, the Reverend shrugged. "We can never be too cautious, so I hope you didn't take offense to my earlier test. But moving forward, tell me exactly what it is you need."

***

Standing by himself, Lance was on the prison's rec yard, watching the inmates compete in a competitive game of five-on-five basketball. A true fan of the sport, he couldn't believe there were people in prison who possessed the skills of professional athletes.

As two men on opposing teams were exchanging trash-talk, which only made the game more exciting to watch, Lance happened to look over his shoulder and saw Cody coming towards him. His heart rate instantly accelerated, for which he inwardly cursed himself. He hated being so fearful, but he didn't know how to cure the loathsome disease.

"What's up, white boy?" Cody greeted in a playful tone, holding out his fist for a pound.

"What's up, Cody?" Lance warily replied, giving him dap. He'd been expecting a confrontation, but not one in such a mild manner.

"Aye, listen, I dug deeper into that one situation, and I found out you was telling the truth. You know, as far as my mans throwing that shit in your shower without telling you what was going on. So that was my fault, lil' nigga."

After learning about the visit between his child's mother and the twins, Cody's investigation had actually been about them. He had asked several savages from Detroit if they were familiar with some twins named Asha and Noni, to which they all answered that they were.

"...And from what they say," one warrior had warned him, "That bitch Noni fight like a man and kill like a marine." Wisely relinquishing his revengeful plan for Lance, Cody instead chose to squash the beef until he could one day obtain the upper hand.

First checking to see if any guards were in the vicinity, Cody pulled a bag of tobacco from inside his pants and offered it to Lance. "Here, put this up. That's enough to fill your locker box up with food, plus some."

As if Cody was trying to hand him a live snake, Lance nervously shook his head in refusal. "Nah, man, I'm good. I just want to do my time and go home."

"You sure?"

Lance nodded, wishing he would hurriedly return the contraband to wherever he had retrieved it. If you found trouble in federal prison and lost 'good days', they were impossible to regain, which led to your out date being pushed back. And Lance had no desire to stay in jail a day longer than necessary.

"Alright, well, let your peoples know everything kosher," Cody said, stuffing the tobacco back in his pants. "And it was just a simple misunderstanding."

After shaking Cody's hand and returning his attention to the game, Lance's thin lips curled into a delighted grin. While he may not have any friends in prison, he sure as hell had some on the streets. And they made sure their presence was felt as if they were physically standing right alongside him.

***

Reverend Daniels led Double-O and Asha to the basement of the Church, where he unlocked a door to a room even his own mother wasn't permitted to enter.

Wrinkling her nose at its musty stench, Asha took in the clutter of antique tables, old cabinets, and a collection of religious-depicted paintings.

With Double-O's help, the Reverend moved aside a large wooden cabinet to reveal a trapdoor in the floor. Double-O and Asha exchanged a brief look before following him down the bunker's staircase.

When the Reverend flicked on an overhead light, he left them spellbound by a scene you only saw in movies.

Arranged in accordance to their size, from micro to massive, attached to a wall were enough weapons to overthrow a small country.

Asha cut her eyes at the Reverend in curiosity, for he clearly wasn't the average religious leader.

Reverend Daniels extended his hand toward the wall. "Take what you like. Ammunition included."

They seized several stainless steel revolvers, over a dozen Glocks of various models, and a handful of high-powered assault rifles. In all, they took down a total of twenty-two guns.

As the Reverend was packing the weapons in duffel bags, Asha removed a roll of rubber-banded money from her coat pocket.

"You haven't mentioned anything about price," she said, laying ten-grand on the table. "So I hope this enough."

He pushed the money away in refusal. "This a favor for a friend."

"Yeah, but you just gave us over twenty guns."

"And he gave me back my freedom," he emphatically replied. "If it wasn't for him, I'd still be a prisoner in purgatory."

Four years ago, before being sentenced to life without parole, Kavoni had indeed delivered $100,000 to the Reverend's mother for the purposes of paying his lawyer fees. Because all crime committed on a state level was basically commercial, the currency had been enough for the Reverend to regain his freedom.

Leaving the money where it lay, Asha grabbed a bag in each hand and stated, "Well, donate it or destroy it. But either way, it won't be leaving with me."

As they were ascending the staircase, Double-O couldn't resist from asking the Reverend a nagging question. "Rev, I know I'm out here living wrong, so I'm always the last to cast judgement. But how do you justify selling guns out of a Church?"

"Well, first of all, I could never justify an intentional sin. I can only hope to offset it. So unlike other shepherds who squeeze the sheep for every penny they can, I use part of my profits to feeds God's flock."

After closing the trapdoor and replacing the cabinet over it, he looked at Double-O and continued, "A man must face and embrace his inner demons. It's the only way to gain a measure of control over his darker half, which we all have. And it's my personal belief that it's not a man's actions that will earn him a seat in God's kingdom, but the condition of his heart. Because surely he'll choose a loyal-hearted sinner over a self-righteous pedophile."

As he let them out through a backdoor, they stashed the bags in the trunk of the car. Asha had picked out a particular pistol for Noni and couldn't wait to witness her reaction upon seeing it.

The Reverend offered them a parting handshake and a reminder on the importance of maintaining balance, which he said the entire world revolved around.

He then turned to personally address Double-O in a menacing tone, "If you run into either of those women before I do, I pray that you'll destroy them to the degree that they rightfully deserve."

As she drove through traffic, Asha glanced at Double-O and nosily inquired, "What women was he referring to?"

"The ones who gave Kavoni a life sentence..." he answered, gazing out the passenger window in deep thought.

"Mecca and Unique."

Chapter 14

"Kiss me!" Angel demanded, as a naked Noni dug into her vaginal orifice with excessive force.

Noni instead slapped her twice in rapid succession.

Her eyes wide with shock and arousal, Angel grabbed Noni by either side of her face and pulled her into a gluttonous kiss. She slept with several men and women in the past, and none could compare to her present partner.

Noni broke the kiss and abruptly withdrew from Angel's volcanic cavity.

"No! no! no!" Angel cried, as she frantically fought to refill her womb with the eight-inch strap-on.

Noni pinned her arms to the bed and converted her cries to moans as she began greedily suckling her breasts like an underfed infant.

"Oh my god!" Angel whined, squirming from tingling sensations that seemed to tickle her spine. No one had ever sucked her breasts with a such a passionate hunger.

Releasing the distended nipple with an audible pop, Noni sat back on her haunches and instructed her to turn over.

She eyed Noni with a desirous look before rolling over to place her face on the pillow and her bottom in the air.

As Noni took a moment to enjoy the scenic view of her provocative pose, a puddle of pudding oozed from within the lips of the prettiest yoni she'd ever encountered.

I gotta get a picture of this, she thought before reaching for her phone.

"What are you doing?" Angel asked, looking over her shoulder.

Noni groaned as she saw a text from her sister, summoning her immediate presence.

"Damn, you should've left this phone alone," she scolded herself.

"I'm sorry, love, but I gotta go," Noni regretfully announced. "It's my sister."

Angel's lips were on the verge of protesting, when Noni captured them in a sensual kiss.

"I promise I'ma make this up to you," she breathed into Angel's greedy mouth. "And next time I'ma torture you for real. 'Cause that wasn't even the appetizer."

As Noni climbed out of bed and began removing her strap, Angel was enchanted by the decorative artwork permanently painted over majority of her body. The most notable being the large butterfly on her back, which was identical to Asha's. She could only imagine the amount of money invested into the elaborate drawings.

"What's Butterfly Mafia?" Angel couldn't refrain from inquiring. The name held a certain appeal that piqued her interest.

Noni smiled as she pulled her hoodie over her head. "If I tell you, I gotta kill you."

"No, seriously, tell me what it is."

She eyed Angel as if deciding whether or not she was trustworthy, then answered, "It's me, my sister, and two of our closest friends. And we each represent a wing that makes up one butterfly."

"So y'all like a sisterhood?" she said in fascination.

Noni nodded. "Something like that."

Quickly crawling to the bed's edge, Angel looked up and earnestly proposed, "I want to be a part of it."

Before Noni could comply or deny, she inserted, "I'm not dumb, Noni. I know you didn't pay for those teeth or tattoos by working a nine-to-five. So believe me when I tell you I can definitely be an asset."

"And how is that?"

"Just look around," she said, waving her hand over the room. "You think my job paying for a place like this? You ain't the only one with secrets."

"So, what's yours?"

Angel got up from the bed and encircled her arms around Noni's neck. "You ever heard of Southwest Perez?"

Noni smirked, thinking of how there wasn't a sinful soul in the city who hadn't heard of Perez. A Mexican drug lord from southwest. He was rumored to be the supplier of every major dealer in the Detroit, Dullah included.

When she nodded in recognition of the name, Angel pecked her lips and revealed, "That's my big brother. Same mother and father. And I'm his only sister, so he gives me anything I want."

Though she was consumed by a feeling more euphoric than when they'd dug up the money, Noni knew her sister would want her to maintain her composure, which is exactly what she did.

"So what, you think you can just buy your way into the Mob?" she asked Angel in an offended tone. "You think we governed by greed, or something?"

"No, that's not what I think at all. Because of what y'all doing for your girl at the rehab, I assume loyalty is more valuable to you than anything else. But I also happen to know that money is power. And the stronger you are, the higher you can climb."

Ecstatic by the endless possibilities Angel's proposal presented, Noni couldn't wait to see her sister. For she already knew Asha would absorb the information and advise them on how to properly proceed. And besides, bringing a Hispanic girl into the picture had been Asha's idea, anyway. It was an additional piece to her masterful plan.

"Listen, I gotta go," Noni said, reaching down to palm handfuls of Angel's soft cheeks. "But I'ma definitely run this pass my twin."

After the two engaged in a long, slow, stirring kiss, Angel vowed in her sincerest voice, "On account of my family's lifestyle, my upbringing revolved around the installation of loyalty. It's who I am. So you would be wise to convince your sister to give me a chance."

Waving goodbye to Angel, who nakedly stood in her doorway, Noni slid behind the wheel of the GTO and sped off.

While en route to the apartment Teer and Double-O shared, her phone began buzzing from an incoming text message.

IMU already! read the text from Angel.

Likewise, Noni texted back. While Angel certainly didn't suffer from a shortage of friends, she was intrigued by Noni and the name Butterfly Mafia. The world was hers in regards to materialism, but she longed to belong to something bigger than herself. So though their butterfly only consisted of four wings, she'd do everything in her power to persuade them that she was worthy of being made an exception.

Checking her rearview mirror before turning into the apartment complex, Noni was certain she wasn't being followed. But still, when she parked beside the Suburban and hopped out, a firearm was fastened to her left hand. It was better to have and not need, than to need and not have.

Upon entering the apartment, Noni's eyes were magnetically drawn to the kitchen table, where a collection of weapons were enticingly resting.

"Damn, Noni!" Asha jokingly scolded her. "Put your tongue back in your mouth and close the door."

"Ohh shit!" she laughed in embarrassment before closing and locking the front door. "I'm on super thirsty shit, huh?"

Walking over to the table of guns, Noni was like a kid in a toy store, not knowing which one to pick out first.

With a hand hidden behind her back, Asha casually approached her indecisive sister. "So, which one you thinking gon' be your favorite?"

"I like this vicious looking joint right here," she said, picking up a P320 Max Pistol. "But you know I like my shit a little more compact."

Knowing exactly what her twin preferred, Asha brought her hand from behind her back. "You mean, something like this?"

Her eyes widened in fascination at the sight of the firearm in her sister's palm. "What the fuck is that?"

The gun in question was a 9mm Hellcat micro compact pistol. It had a three-inch barrel, built-in red beam, and a standard 13-round magazine. This was a pocket rocket with power.

Eagerly exchanging the P320 for the Hellcat, Noni cradled it with delicacy as if it was a prematurely born baby.

She had a sudden thought and looked up from the gun to her sister, "You got this just for me, didn't you?"

Asha smiled at the other half of her heart and soul. "As soon as I saw it, I could picture your reaction. So there was no way I was leaving without it."

She loved Noni beyond description and would do nearly anything to please and protect her.

As the two sisters embraced for an extended period of time, Double-O joked, "Yo, I swear, for y'all to be as dangerous as y'all is, y'all some emotional ass women!"

After stashing majority of their arsenal in an attic, they gathered in the front room and Noni informed them of Angel's proposal.

"And she said Perez her blood brother?" Lo-Lo asked in mild disbelief. She'd once saw the drug lord when he came to the club at which she danced and donated nearly six figures.

Noni nodded. "I mean, she do gotta plush ass condo downtown. And ain't no way no receptionist job paying for that. So she gotta have something going on."

As the group continued to debate the probability of Angel's kinship to a kingpin, Asha rose from the couch and went over to the window, where she gazed up at the star lit sky. She rubbed her palms on her pants, as they had begun to sweat from the rush of adrenaline.

Their chatter receded into a curious silence as they took in Asha standing over at the window.

"What's the matter, love?" Lo-Lo inquired in a concerned tone.

Asha turned from the window with a joyful glow. "Don't y'all see... everything is lining up. We're literally being given everything we need to get ahead. So there's no doubt in my mind that this Angel girl will help accelerate our growth."

Recalling something someone had recently told her, Asha encouragingly added, "So from here on out, let's start seeing the glass as half full."

Chapter 15

Attending their very first football game, the Mob followed Angel to a Skybox at the Detroit Lions stadium. With the home team competing against Aaron Rogers and his Green Bay Packers, the volume inside the arena was deafening, as it was packed to its capacity with diehard fans.

Outside the Skybox stood two security guards, who wore cargo pants and militant stances. One was a Conan built male, and the other a women with thighs the size of a running back's.

After the three girls were frisked by the woman before having the man wave a wire detecting wand over their bodies, Angel was then permitted to lead her guests into the luxurious room.

"Are you fucking kidding me, ref!" a man screamed in frustration as he stood before a large window. "That was clearly a pass interference!"

As he continued to rant and rave at a referee who was unable to even hear him, Angel offered them a drink from a miniature bar.

Asha declined on behalf of all three. While the setting may have been sociable, the affair was strictly business. "But you can give us some bottled waters, if you got 'em."

Their every move was being monitored by a Central American, who sat deathly still on a barstool in a corner of the room. He bore the eyes of a tiger, with gang graffiti sprayed over his head and face. An MS-13 originally from El Salvador, he'd march down on the field and murder the referee at just the snap of his boss's finger.

When the man's screaming subsided and he turned from the window, Lo-Lo immediately recognized him as being the same charitable character from that night at the club.

And just as it had on that eventful occasion, his presence reeked of power and prosperity.

"So these are the friends you've been telling me about," Perez smiled, reaching out to shake either of their hands.

"And you must be Noni," he said upon shaking hers.

To her surprised reaction, he replied, "You gotta tell me some of your secrets. Because whatever you've done, my little sister hasn't been able to stop talking about you."

Her cheeks reddening in embarrassment, Angel playfully shoved him. "Brother!"

"What?" he held up his hands in mock innocence. "I'm just telling it like it is."

After refilling his drink, Perez took a seat and instructed for the girls to follow suit.

"You have a very businesslike demeanor," he said to Asha, peering directly into her eyes. "So, I'll bypass the small talk and get straight to it."

Downing his drink in a single gulp, he uncrossed his legs and leaned forward. "I've never dealt with female dealers for two factual reasons. One, they're likely to be seen as easy targets to robbery crews. And two, they're even more likely to have loose lips inside an interrogation room. History is known for repeating itself, so what makes you three any different?"

Asha leaned forward and replied, "One, we'll murder any amount of men foolish enough to fuck with our food. And two, we've already sat inside that room. We'd cut out our own tongues before we ever sunk to the level of rats."

Perez pleasingly nodded at her response, then made a startling statement that meant he had done his homework. "I'm aware of the time y'all did in juvie."

Maintaining a neutral mentality, Asha replied, "But what you don't know is that had we not sat in silence, we'd still be in that cage."

At the ages of seventeen, the three girls had taken police on a high speed chase. Upon Lo-Lo crashing into the living room of an unoccupied house, authorities found a large amount of drugs and several firearms in the trunk. But what they hadn't known was that the seized items were stolen from Noni's first murder victim.

"And while that may certainly be true," Perez remarked, "That still isn't enough to instill the skill and experience required to ward off the wolves. Because at the smell of fresh meat, they'll definitely come sniffing around. And there's a big difference between doing time and taking a life. One requires a bit more—"

"Not to cut you off," Noni interrupted. "But I done put more heads to bed than a daycare. And I mean that literally. So don't think just because we girls we can't get gritty."

Perez smirked. "Does Dullah know you're here?"

Even Asha was caught off guard by his unexpected inquiry.

"There's not much I don't know about," Perez continued, "Especially when it directly involves me, or my loved ones."

"We don't work for Dullah no more," Asha informed him. "We're on our own now."

"And why is that?"

"With all due respect, I'd rather not speak on that. But just know that it had nothing to do with flaws in either of our characters."

Having provided the proper response, Perez questioned her in regards to what exactly they were looking to purchase.

"We wanted to mix it up, between meth and fentanyl."

"And how much are you planning to invest?"

After paying for the guns and providing her peoples with pocket change, that left them with roughly... "We got $35,000 to our name. And we're willing to invest it all."

While wearing a thoughtful expression, he could feel his sister's brown eyes pinning him with a pleading stare.

"Here's what I can offer," Perez soon proposed, gazing directly at Noni. "There's a guy who owes me just under ninety grand. But I'm no longer concerned about the money. So, in exchange for his life, I'll give you the amount of his debt in the drugs you want."

"Say less," Noni agreed without a moment's hesitation. If Perez needed proof of her savagery, she'd happily provide it.

"But there's one condition," he inserted.

"Which is?"

"That there be witnesses. I want this to be a warning that excuses are intolerable when pertaining to business."

"And can we consider this as part of a payment towards a partnership fee?" Asha wisely inquired. "Because we intend to use our profit return for further investment."

Pouring himself another generous amount of Patron, Perez peered over the brim of his glass and promised, "Should you issue this warning in a timely manner... I'll personally see to it that you become the Queenpin of Detroit."

***

Several days later, Teer was steering a stolen sedan through the city's east side. With Double-O riding shotgun and Noni in the backseat, both passengers were palming pistols equipped with circular drums containing fifty Critical Duty rounds.

"We getting busy at the next light," Noni announced, as they trailed a Mercedes Benz from three car lengths. "Fuck all that waiting shit."

Checking his side mirror as he activated his blinker, Teer slid over into the adjacent lane and sped up.

After nearly a week of surveillance, they discovered an afternoon pattern, in which their target faithfully followed. Subsequent to a workout at a fitness gym, he would stop for a high protein salad before being chauffeured back to his residence out in Birmingham. While the initial plan was to ambush him on the expressway, Noni had made the mistake of growing impatient.

In the backseat of the Benz, the target was curiously staring at the darkly tinted car travelling beside him. He could make out the silhouette of three people, but nothing more. As his mind strangely thought of the outstanding debt he owed his drug connect, the truck came to a stop at a traffic light.

The man was on the verge of yelling for his driver to burn rubber, when both windows on the car's passenger side simultaneously lowered.

As Double-O extended his arm and hammered the two up front with hollows to their helmets, Noni bit down on her bottom lip and fired multiple rounds into the backseat area.

Amid the chaotic sounds of screeching tires and blaring horns, Noni threw on her hood and hopped out the car.

"What the fuck is she doing?" Teer shouted in panic.

"A thorough job," Double-O calmly answered, as he attentively watched her like a BMF episode.

As the bullet riddled car coasted across the intersection, Noni stuck her arm into the backseat, where the fearful-eyed target was coughing up blood.

"This from Perez," she said, then leaned in closer and put an end to his suffering.

When she jumped back in the car and Teer rounded the corner with a loud screech, a cruiser followed suit just seconds later.

Upon activation of its overhead lights, which Noni referred to as 'cherries and berries', the cruiser surged forward and began closing the distance.

"Drive this muthafucka!" Double-O barked, nervously staring at his side mirror. He couldn't imagine returning to I-Max with a life sentence.

As Noni kept turning in her seat to keep an eye on the closeness of the cop car, she cursed herself for not sticking to the original plan. Frightened by the sudden thought of being physically separated from her sibling, her mind began frantically thinking of how to evade capture.

In spite of his expert driving, as he raced down alleyways and residential streets, Teer was unable to lose the cruiser.

"We gotta get out on foot!" Noni advised, as she witnessed a second cruiser join in on the chase. "This bitch ain't fast enough."

Bending a left at the next side street, Teer slammed on the brakes and they hopped out, dashing in different directions.

As Noni ran between two houses, she glanced over her shoulder and saw to her dismay that a male officer was in full pursuit.

"Think, Noni, think!" she screamed at herself in desperation. Had she not abandoned her gun in the car, she could've shot in the air as a means of slowing him down.

When she reached for the top of a wooden fence and went to pull herself over it, the officer withdrew his weapon and fired several times.

Groaning in pain as she tumbled to the ground on the other side of the fence, fear and adrenaline enabled her to spring back up and resume running.

With a stinging sensation in her lower left leg, Noni knew she needed to hide. The gunshot wound had slowed her pace, and it wouldn't be long before the cop was able to catch up to her and finish the job. And with her being a suspect in a triple murder, her death would definitely be ruled as justified.

Wearing a painful grimace as she climbed over another fence, she couldn't believe her luck, when a barking Rottweiler came charging toward her. Not knowing what to do but stare it down, she sighed in slight relief as the canine stopped short and started to growl.

"Please, don't bite me, doggy," she softly pled, while limping her way across the lawn. Noni had noticed something that gave her a hopeful idea.

As the Rottweiler watched her with an inquisitive eye, Noni got down on her and knees and crawled inside the dog's house.

When, moments later, the male officer landed in the backyard with a loud thud, the dog turned from Noni and greeted him in the same barking manner.

Just as the officer withdrew his weapon in preparation to shoot the dog, the back porch light blinked on a drew his attention.

"What's going on out there?" an older black woman asked the officer through her screen door. "And Missy, go to your house!"

As the dog reluctantly obeyed, which blocked the view of Noni's curled up frame, the officer replaced the weapon in his holster and explained that he was in pursuit of a murder suspect.

"Well, you won't find 'em back there," she assured him, "Because Missy don't tolerate no strangers coming into her backyard."

After a brief glance around the yard, and at the snarling dog, he apologized for the inconvenience and exited the backyard.

The woman was on the verge of closing her door, when she noticed that Missy was no longer growling, but intently focused on something inside her dog house.

She considered calling out to the officer but thought better of it upon having a sudden realization. If Missy had allowed something or someone to enter her beloved house, then surely there was nothing to be afraid of.

"What my Missy looking at, huh?" the woman sang while approaching the dog.

When she bent down to peer inside, she gasped in surprise at the sight of Noni, whose wide eyes were filled with fear.

Nervously looking over her shoulder, the woman turned back to Noni and whispered in urgency, "Girl, what you doing in there? Don't you know you could've gotten Missy killed?"

"I'm sorry, ma'am, but I'm in trouble," Noni admitted. "And I promise you, if he catch me, he gon' kill me. He already shot me."

"I'm sorry, too, but you can't stay in there."

"Well, ma'am, can you please call my sister and tell her where I am? I can't run no more."

The woman cut her eyes at Missy with a scolding expresson, and the dog guiltily lowered her head. She knew she was to supposed to protect the yard, but her canine senses had told her the intruder wasn't a threat.

"What's the number?" the woman sighed in consent, removing a phone from the pocket of her robe.

Asha answered the call in a hesitant voice, "Hello?"

"Twin, it's me," Noni said in relief.

"Girl, where are you!?"

"Child, you gotta lower your voice now," the woman cut in. "Cause I got you on this here speaker phone. And the po-lice is crawling around here like cockroaches."

"Yes, ma'am, I'm sorry," Asha said in a lowered tone. "But that's my twin sister, and I was just so worried about her."

"I understand," the woman nodded, then gave her their location.

After disconnecting the call, the woman encouraged Noni to change the lifestyle that led to her present predicament. "Because if I plant collard green seeds in my garden, then I can't expect mustards to grow out the ground. And it's the same with life. We can only get out what we put in. And remember, God can't lie."

Not long after the woman went inside the house, taking Missy with her, Noni saw the porch light blink on and off.

Crawling out the dog house, she rose to her feet and hurriedly limped around to the front of the house, where Asha sat behind the wheel of the GTO.

"Damn, what happened?" she asked in concern, as Noni slouched inside the car with a painful groan.

"Cocksucker got me somewhere in the leg," she breathlessly answered. "Twin, I swear I ain't never been that damn scared in all my life."

The sisters enveloped each other in a fierce embrace before Asha pulled off.

When she came to a stop at a traffic light, she had Noni raise her pant leg so she could inspect her injury. Upon doing so, they were relieved to discover that it was only a flesh wound and didn't require immediate medical attention.

"Girl, he only grazed you," Asha smiled, playfully pushing her. "And here I am thinking you gotta go to the 'spital."

"Man, the way it was burning, I swear it felt like he blew my shit clean off."

While impatiently waiting for the light to change, Asha began wrinkling her nose at the sudden smell of a foul odor. "What the fuck is that smell?"

Sniffing the air, Noni caught a whiff of it herself and began checking her clothing as the possible source.

When she lifted up in her seat, Asha laughingly pointed at a large stain on the back of her left leg. "Girl, you got dog shit all over your ass!"

Noni could only join in on the laughter. Because had it not been for the Rottweiler named Missy, she would've likely ended up in the city morgue or the county jail.

Chapter 16

Inside an abandoned Duplex on Seven-Mile, three men were doing construction work on the building's second floor. And while they bore the skills and efficiency of licensed employees, they were actually drug addicts who preferred to be paid in shards of Meth.

After four days of twelve hour shifts, the lead worker removed his gloves and made a brief phone call. "Come check it out."

Twenty minutes later, Lo-Lo and Asha entered the building through its backdoor.

"This was more work than I thought," the lead worker admitted, as he led them to the apartment upstairs. His name Randy, he was the eldest brother of Lo-Lo's late mother.

When Lo-Lo was greeted by the two coworkers as they entered the kitchen, she gave partial hugs to her first cousins, Ronnie and Roland.

"So does anything look out of place?" Randy asked, waving his hand over the kitchen.

Lo-Lo and Asha looked around before shaking their heads.

Flashing a pleased smile, Randy pulled the refrigerator away from the wall to expose a trap door that measured four feet in height.

"It'll open with just a push," he informed, doing so to show them the simplicity of it. "Then once you're inside, you can grab this lever on the refrigerator right here and pull it back against the wall."

After explaining how the secret compartment could take you to either the apartment below or the rooftop, he led them downstairs to the building's backdoor. "We reinforced the frame and did the same in front. So if the spot was to ever get raided, it'll give you plenty of time to make it upstairs and get rid of whatever evidence you need to. And you can open this slot here on the door by simply sliding over the latch."

The slot he referred to was in the center of the back-door. It would serve as the precautionary means of all drug deals that were to soon take place. So while there would be hand-to-hand transactions, there would be no visuals of who was behind the door. And with iron bars welded over the first floor windows, the building was basically like a fortress.

Incorporating her own ideas with techniques from the past, Asha had decided to open up a trap house that dealt two separate drugs. The building would be open around the clock, with workers doing eight hour shifts. They would be paid $200 from every $1,000 made. And to ensure that they couldn't catch a lengthy sentence if arrested, she would employ no one over the age of seventeen.

Handsomely rewarding Lo-Lo's people for their services, Asha gave them each a pound of Meth, along with a subtle warning to maintain secrecy.

Barely able to contain their excitement as they sped off in the Suburban, the two girls held hands. "I can't believe how everything coming together!" Lo-Lo beamed, briefly removing her eyes from the road.

"I know, right?" Asha smiled before leaning over to kiss Lo-Lo on the cheek. "And just think... this only the beginning."

***

From his slouched position in the backseat of the car, Double-O was looking up front at Noni with an inward feeling of admiration and respect. The girl had more heart than half the men he'd met. And he had stood alongside some real live savages.

"Noni, you could be a movie character," Teer looked at her from the passenger seat, as she left-handedly steered them through traffic. "I'm saying, you whoop shit, kill more niggas than the police, and now you out here getting shot and hiding in dog houses. Yeah, if you ask me, that's definitely some movie shit."

"Double-O, you hear this lil nigga?" Noni laughed, gripping the wheel in one hand and her micro Hellcat in the other. "He ready to start filming this shit. And they gon' have our ass in Pelican Bay. SHU program, nigga. Twenty-four-hour lockdown!"

They all laughed at her impersonation of Denzel Washington in the movie Training Day.

While it wasn't humorous at the time, they could now jokingly reminisce on their close encounter with law enforcement. And though Teer and Double-O's foot chase hadn't been as eventful as Noni's, they had also narrowly escaped capture.

Turning into a Jiffy Lube, Noni lowered the music as she drove up to its service entry.

When a courtesy technician the height of an N.B.A. player approached the car, Double-O leaned up from the backseat.

"Ohhh shit!" the man raised his fist to his mouth in surprise. "My nigga, Double-O. When you get out, my baby?"

His nickname CJ, shortened from Car Jack, he was an original member of Double-O's former crew. Famous for his speed and efficiency at Grand Theft Auto, he had once peeled the column of an eighteen wheeler.

After saying he'd been out for a couple of months, Double-O jutted his chin at CJ's workplace. "So how you liking it?"

With his hands wedged in his pants pockets, CJ shrugged, "It's paying the bills, man. I mean, clearly I want more. But slow motion better than no motion, right? And before I crash out and go back in that cage, I'd rather do oil changes and tire rotations."

They all had to nod in respect at CJ's perspective.

"You still trust me?" Double-O questioned one of his closest comrades.

"Wholeheartedly," CJ answered without hesitation.

Double-O nudged his head in invitation. "Well, hop in."

CJ held his friend's stare for a moment, then turned to face his place of employment.

"Fuck it," he decided before turning to march to the manager's office.

When CJ reappeared minutes later, he was wearing his own clothing and walking a mountain bike.

Noni frowned as him and the Mongoose approached her side of the car. "What the fuck is that?"

"My ride to work," CJ answered.

"And what, you trying to put that mu'fucka in my trunk, or something?"

"I mean, if that's cool with you."

Noni turned to Double-O and aimed her thumb at his friend. "Is this nigga for real right now?"

Before he could answer, she spun back on CJ and said, "Boy, if you ghost-ride that bitch across the parking lot and come the fuck on!"

After laughingly doing as told, CJ climbed in the backseat and Noni exited his former job site with a loud squeal.

"So what's up with that nigga, Smurf?" Double-O asked CJ, as they rode through traffic.

He scoffed in disgust at the mention of the name. "Man, dog changed up on me like the weather. He found a plug from somewhere right after you got locked up, and he got brand new on a nigga."

Recalling the fortune and fame his crew had once attained, CJ shook his head and continued, "After King died and you went to the joint, wasn't no more unity or structure. Niggas started veering off, doing their own thing. So, I did what I had to do and got a job."

CJ had the heart of a lion, but the soul of a soldier. Like many, he wasn't built to lead. But if presented with a plan he perceived as possible, he'd follow a friend with utter integrity.

Upon their reentry into the inner city, Teer popped off the inside door panel and removed three Ziplock bags of drugs from the secret compartment.

CJ couldn't help but curiously peer up front as Teer withdrew individual baggies and capsules from inside each bag.

"Here," Teer said, passing a Ziplock bag over the seat to Double-O.

CJ bumped him with his elbow and nudged his head at the bag.

"You can talk, my baby," Double-O smiled. "But these testers. We got that Vanilla Ice, and young Fetty Wap. And we gon' ride around and pass these mu'fuckas out all over the city."

After Noni issued the publicized warning, which Perez pleasingly referred to as a 3-for-1 special, he gave them pounds of meth and a half key of raw fentanyl. And with his promise to provide them with a steady supply, they would ensure each tester recipient that their product would never be mild, tainted, or diluted. But more importantly, they'd let it be known that their trap house like Wayne County Jail, for it was always open.

Later that night, after passing out hundreds of testers and the address of their duplex, they pulled up to the house in which CJ currently lived.

"Who spot is this?" Double-O asked on a hunch.

"It's a lil' boarding house," CJ admitted in embarrassment. "You know, just something till I can get on my feet."

Saddened by his friend's current living conditions, Double-O told Noni to pull off.

"Hold up!" CJ grabbed the back of her seat. "I gotta grab my clothes and shit real quick."

"Bro, don't worry about none of that," Double-O waved a dismissive hand. "We'll take you to the mall tomorrow. I can't speak for nobody else, but I got you, my baby. I already know where your heart at."

CJ just looked at him as there were no words to express his love and appreciation. But it felt unbelievably good to have a true friend in his corner.

Inside Double-O and Teer's two-bedroom apartment - where CJ was welcomed to live with open arms, Double-O told him to make do with the couch until they could find a bigger place.

"I really appreciate this, bro," CJ said in genuine gratitude. "You was always like a brother to me. And I just want you to know that I'll never take your friendship for granted."

As the two friends shook hands and embraced, Double-O assured him, "It might be just us two right now, but we still The F.A.M., my baby."

His teeth shining bright, a smiling CJ bobbed his head in agreement, "The Few Against Many."

Chapter 17

Inside the idling Suburban, Lo-Lo and Noni quietly chatted up front, while Asha was in the backseat, busily typing on a laptop. They were parked down the street from their 24-hour trap house. And despite it being close to midnight, drug addicts were still arriving in droves.

In her strategic thinking, Asha had chosen a building on a block of primarily abandoned houses. The less neighbors, the less complaints there would be about the amount of traffic the building attracted.

"It's crazy how hard this bitch jumping already," Noni commented, watching as both genders were marching around to the back of the building.

"And it's only been a week!" Lo-Lo chimed in. "So just think how much harder it's gon' go once the word spreads. Because if it's one thing I learned from my mama, it's that a mu'fucka will walk all the way from Flint for some good dope."

In the backseat, Asha's features were illuminated by the glow of her MacBook. Intently focused on the screen, her fingers would occasionally fly over its keyboard.

"How's it coming along, love?" Lo-Lo asked, turning in her seat.

Asha nodded without looking up, "I'm almost done."

Purchasing 'profiles' from the dark web, which consisted of a person's social and address, she selected the profiles of recently deceased women with perfect credit scores. She then used that information to create a phony LLC for each person. If the next step went well, which depended on Lo-Lo, Asha was certain they'd soar to a peak only few had ever reached.

Riding a bicycle, a hooded figure emerged from on the side of the building and came pedaling down the block. The cyclist casually scanned the area before veering towards the Suburban.

Lo-Lo lowered the driver side window as Teer's youthful face came into view.

"What up, doe?" he greeted, as he rode up to the truck and laid a hand on the roof for balance.

As they returned the greeting, Teer removed a small bag from the front pouch of his hoodie and dropped it on Lo-Lo's lap. "That's a little over seven racks."

To prevent the accumulation of too much money inside the apartment, Asha had wisely decided to do daily pickups. So whether the spot was raided or robbed, they'd suffer only a small loss.

Reaching beneath her seat, Lo-Lo grabbed a package and passed it to Teer. "That should hold you for the next few days," she said, as he tucked it beneath his hoodie.

On account of her familiarity with hard drugs, Lo-Lo was in charge of their narcotics division. She oversaw everything from dilution to distribution. Smart enough to have been a math teacher, she kept a mental record of every gram given to Teer and his team.

"A'ight, I'll see y'all tomorrow," Teer double tapped the roof before pedaling back toward the building. With him being just sixteen, he occasionally found it hard to believe he'd been appointed to a position his peers practically prayed to attain.

As Lo-Lo pulled off, they drove pass a navy blue Cutlass, in which Double-O and CJ attentively sat. With their gloved hands holding fully automatics, their job was to watch for wolves while the women collected the money.

But in spite of the girls moving with a great deal of caution, there was an opposing force presently working against them.

**

Gripping a stack of singles in one hand and a champagne bottle in the other, Pierre was all smiles as an exotic dancer grinded on him in the VIP booth of a strip club. This was a luxury he could yet afford and was thoroughly enjoying.

Seated across from him was Smurf, the alleged friend who'd been generous enough to fund the event. A regular attendant at the club, he observed Pierre with a humored glint.

"What up, you trying to take her home?" Smurf asked Pierre over the loud music.

When Pierre eyed him as if he was joking, Smurf laughingly assured him, "Nigga, I'm serious. Now, do you want her, or what?"

"Hell yeah!" Pierre emphatically answered. "This the baddest bitch I ever seen."

Once the dance ended, Smurf showed the woman five Franklins before handing them to Pierre. "Give my lil mans your number and he gon' give you that bread when y'all link up later tonight."

Scribbling her name and number on a napkin, she made sure to leave Pierre with a memorable visual of her vibrant bottom as she sashayed off.

"That's good looking, big homie!" Pierre exclaimed, reaching over the table to shake Smurf's hand. "And I promise you, I'ma fuck the shit out that lil pretty ass bitch. She gon' fuck around and tell me to keep the money!"

Smurf smiled in amusement. "I hear you, lil nigga. Just make sure you enjoy yourself, 'cause that's why I did it. Don't think I ain't noticed how loyal you've been over these past few months."

Since befriending the younger man, Smurf had been taking advantage of his indigent situation. He'd sent Pierre on a number of missions, ranging from dangerous to drug related, and he loved how the boy never complained about being paid peanuts. And this what he was referring to as "loyalty."

Filled with emotion from the effects of alcohol, Pierre slurred in a sentimental tone, "You the realest nigga I ever met, big homie. You know I ain't got nobody, and you made a way for me to eat. So it'll always be all love on my end. And I'd do anything to prove my loyalty. All you gotta do is ask."

It was a quarter after 2AM, when Smurf led a staggering Pierre outside to the car. "Come on, lil' nigga, I gotta get you to the crib before you fuck around and pass out."

"Nah, my baby," Pierre protested, "I gotta hit ol' girl up. I'm trying to fuck her to death, you hear me?"

"Man, get with that hoe tomorrow," Smurf suggested, helping him into the passenger seat of his Silverado. "Because you too drunk right now to do anything but go to sleep."

Had Pierre not been so caught up in the moment, he would've saw that Smurf sipped on the same bottle throughout the night.

As they headed to the projects where Pierre lived, Smurf looked over to see his eye lids on the verge of closing. "So did I show you a good time, or what?" he yelled, jarring the drunken man back to life.

Pierre lazily smiled. "Dog... I ain't have that much fun on my birthday. Nigga, we had the booth, the bottles, and all the bitches. I definitely gotta get my cake up. 'Cause I'm trying to go hard like that every weekend."

After a brief lapse of silence, Smurf casually asked him, "Aye, did you ever get a chance to watch the video of that shit that happened at Belle Isle?"

"Did I?" Pierre replied. "Shit, I was probably one of the first. I seen that shit the same morning it got posted."

"Nigga, that was some wild ass shit. But what's even rawer is that don't nobody know who did it. 'Cause I'm in these streets faithfully, and even I ain't heard not one name mentioned."

Due to the impairment of mind, Pierre fell for the bait and turned to face Smurf with a proud smirk. "I don't know about nobody else, but I know who did it. I just ain't said shit."

Smurf met his gaze with a doubtful one. "You know who did it?"

"Hell yeah," Pierre affirmed with conviction.

"Who?"

Thinking Smurf was a friend with whom he could share a secret, Pierre answered, "Between me and you, it was my home girls, Asha and Noni."

Although he'd heard the names being associated with violence, Smurf feigned disbelief to uncover more information. "Man, ain't no way you expect me to believe that two bitches put down no vicious move like that. Yeah, let me hurry up and drop your drunk ass off. 'Cause now you start taking me for a fool."

"Nah, for real, big homie, they off the chain for real. Matter fact, Noni just boxed a nigga in the projects a few weeks ago. In front of everybody. They argued on a Tuesday, and that nigga was dead before the following Tuesday."

"But what that gotta do with what happened at Belle Isle?"

Pierre explained that he initially began to suspect the twins, when Noni showed more concern than surprise over seeing the video. Then, when learning the names and M.O. of the two victims, he recalled the home invasion that claimed their mother's life a few years back. Instinctively putting two-and-two together, he watched the video more closely.

"I've been around 'em since we was kids," Pierre continued. "And I could just tell it was Noni by her body movements. Not to mention, the shooter was left-handed, and so are the twins. And if that ain't enough, just look at the feet. They small as hell... like a girl's."

Despite the fact that his story held a ring of truth, Smurf doubtfully replied, "Yeah, I hear you, but I don't know if I'm buying that. I mean, it's possible, but I don't see it. But whoever did it, they some vicious mu'fuckas."

Turning into the Brewster Projects, Smurf was on high alert as he took in a group of hooligans hanging out in the courtyard. This was an area known for its excessive violence, which meant the loiterers likely had larceny on their minds.

"Alright, I'ma get up with you in a minute, lil' bruh," he shook Pierre's hand, anxious for him to exit the truck.

"Alright, big homie."

Pierre was slowly climbing out, when he turned back to ask if he should return the money. "You know, since I ain't get a chance to hook up with ol' girl."

"Nah, you good," Smurf waved his hand. "You can call her later or spend that shit on whatever."

No sooner than Pierre shut the door, Smurf sped off without caring to see if he safely entered his apartment.

Glancing at his rearview mirror as he exited the projects, Smurf couldn't believe his luck. Because not only had he managed to fulfill Mecca's request, but it only costed a trip to the strip club and $500.

Chapter 18

Lo-Lo wore a pinstripe pantsuit and Manola Blahnik mules as she marched into a bank with an air of authority. Carrying a leather attaché case, she was disguised in a dark wig, and a pair of chic lenses over brown eye contacts.

"Hi, how may I help you?" Politely asked a female teller.

"Yes, I'm here to see Mr. Fitzgerald. I have a 1 o'clock appointment."

After making a brief phone call, the teller informed Lo-Lo that he'd be right with her.

Minutes later, the manager emerged from a back office. He was a short, balding man with an obvious affection for food.

"I'm Ms. Tannerhill," Lo-Lo shook his hand. "We recently spoke over the phone."

"Ah, yes," he smiled in recollection. "If you'll follow me."

He showed her to a small office, where he took seat behind his desk and interlocked his pudgy hands. "If I remember correctly, I believe you were interested in opening up a business account."

"And you would be correct," Lo-Lo said, removing the necessary documents from her leather case. In her preparation of this moment, Asha had made sure that everything was proper.

"And what sort of business are we referring to?"

"Adult entertainment."

"Oh," he replied, with a slight reddening of his cheeks. With her business like demeanor and attire, he'd been caught off guard.

"Me and my ex-husband had got into the business several years ago," Lo-Lo explained. "As you can probably imagine, the profits were significant. But after a bitter divorce, and my own ignorance, he was able to walk away with the entire company. So I've basically had to start over. And here I am."

"And what is the name of your company?"

"Cash Yoni Productions."

Asha had chosen the porn business on account of it being a billion dollar industry. And with Lo-Lo being an attractive white girl, who claimed to have already co-owned a company, it was logical to believe that she would generate a ton of revenue, which made for great banking business.

After presenting the manager with business documents and various forms of identification, she was elated to hear that a business account would be made active within the next hour.

As they were on the verge of leaving the office, Lo-Lo smacked her forehead in forgetfulness. "Silly me," she smiled, withdrawing a cashier's check from her purse. "I'd like to deposit this into my account."

"Yes, ma'am, I'll see that it's taken care of," he happily assured her, taking in the check for the amount of $10,000.

Another one of Asha's bright ideas, the check was to establish a sense of trust. But more importantly, it was an investment that would accelerate their financial growth.

Exiting the bank, Lo-Lo slid into the backseat of a Ford Fusion.

"Where to?" her Uber driver inquired.

"The Chase bank, downtown on Third."

Unable to contain her excitement, Lo-Lo grabbed her phone and sent Asha a short text, accompanied by a smiley emoji.

One down, three to go.

***

Asha was walking into a Jamaican restaurant, when she received Lo-Lo's text message. She smiled to herself while sending the reply,

Cali', here we come!

Her spirits were instantly dampened by the sight of the person seated at a booth in back of the restaurant. But knowing the importance of masking her emotions, Asha approached the table with an unreadable half-smile.

"Thank you for coming," Dullah said, rising to greet her with a handshake. "And I'll try not to take up too much of your time."

Dullah had recently contacted Asha and asked if they could sit down and talk, alone. Only after he agreed to meet in a public place did she grant his request. And while she had no intentions on complying with whatever proposal he would surely present, she wanted to appear cordial until the time came to crush his can.

"You should try the Jerk Chicken," Dullah suggested before biting into a piece of his own. "This shit so good it should be illegal."

I don't know what my mama saw in this nigga, Asha thought to herself in disgust. Just because a man had murdered a few people and collected a few coins didn't exclude him from being a clown. And in Dullah's case, the man should invest in his own circus.

Complaining of cramps, Asha declined. She was there on business and would give no indication that it was anything else.

After scarfing down his meal with the manners of a wild dog, Dullah pushed his plate aside and spoke, "I gotta proposal for you."

"And what's that?" Asha boredly inquired.

"I want to set you up in that weed spot you was talking about. After thinking it over, I realized you was right. It wouldn't be hard for you to make it happen. And not to come off on no creep shit, but your looks would definitely help boost your clientele with these thirsty ass niggas. Because once they find out it's a pretty face selling it, they'll go broke to convince you that they out here balling."

Asha had to admit that the clown did just make it make sense. But it was too late. And another thing, during his spiel he repeatedly used the word "you", rather than "y'all". Knowing she came as a package deal. Knowing she'd choose death over disloyalty any day of the week. Especially when it came to Noni.

"Dullah, I appreciate it, but I'ma have to pass. Because after our last meeting, I didn't know how shit was gon' play out. So I started looking for another route and found it."

"Come on, Asha, you know I wasn't gon' leave you for dead, girl. But your sister just be —"

"Don't speak on Noni. For one, she ain't here. And for two, you should know I'll never go against her."

"You right, you right," he held up his hands in apology. "But I'm just saying, don't let something so small interfere with us making power moves. Because I'm telling you, Asha, as a team we could take over this city. We'd be unstoppable. I just need you to trust me on this one. And I promise you and your sister will have them six figures you was talking about."

As Asha listened to the plea in his voice, she now realized how fortunate she was that Dullah had initially shut her down. Because had he not, she would've never encountered the pressure that enabled her to approach the drawing board with a sense of urgency.

"Dullah, I don't doubt a word you just said. But like I told you, I'm already committed to something else now."

"I'm saying, what could you possibly have going on that outweighs what I'm bringing to the table?"

Asha could see that he was becoming increasingly agitated, and she was beginning to question her decision in agreeing to this meeting. Some men were governed by emotion, which made them difficult to deal with. Especially when it concerned cutting ties.

"I need you to understand something, Dullah," Asha leaned forward and gave him direct eye contact. "You not my man or my father. And you've never given me nothing for free. Every dime you've ever paid me, I earned. So what I got going on is my business, and I'm not obligated to discuss it with nobody but the people involved. And if you can't respect that, then I don't know what else to tell you."

Clenching his jaw in anger, Dullah replied, "When y'all came home from the joint on some hungry shit, with your tongues hanging out, it was me who put food on your fucking plate. And after they killed your mama and raped your sister, it was me that found out who did it. So don't you ever fix your fucking lips to say you don't owe me."

Despite maintaining a calm demeanor, Asha was fuming on the inside. And if she'd been in possession of a weapon right then, she would've turned his plate into his pillow. But refusing to reward him with the satisfaction of seeing her ruffled, Asha maintained a poker face as she stood up.

"Clearly, I thought we could sit down and have a civilized conversation. But clearly I was wrong. Because for you to try and attack me on a personal level, just because I won't do what you want, just tells me how you really feel."

"And for the record," she added very clearly, "Me and my sister never admitted to doing nothing to nobody. We put the past behind us and moved on. And I advise you to do the same."

"Fuck that supposed to mean?" Dullah sprung to his feet with a menacing scowl. "You know I don't take kindly to threats."

"I wish you could see how you look right now," Asha shook her head in contempt. "And don't think I don't know what this is really about. Because this shit deeper than what you making it out to be."

"I don't know what the fuck you talking about," he blinked, which was a sign that implied otherwise.

Knowing her words had struck a nerve, Asha smirked, "Sure you don't."

Even when her mother was alive, Asha had noticed the way Dullah would watch her. And the fact that she did nothing to entice him only seemed to heighten his indecent desire. She had hoped it would fizzle out over time, but his current behavior showed that the obsession had grown. To the point where he'd rather see her starve if not in his arms.

As she turned to walk away, Dullah called out, "If you leave, ain't no coming back!"

Without turning, Asha threw up the peace sign and kept it moving. Before she went back to Dullah, she'd go back to jail.

Asha was driving down the street, replaying her and Dullah's conversation, when she suddenly slammed on her brakes, nearly causing a collision with the car behind her. The twins had never told anyone about what happened to Noni on the night of the home invasion. So, how had Dullah known about it? But more interestingly, how had he really known who the two men were?

Trembling in rage and alarm as she slowly pulled off, Asha knew these were questions that could only be answered by Dullah himself. And she'd inflict whatever amount of torture it took to convince him to comply.

Chapter 19

A Month Later...

"I'm everywhere comfortable, but I'm still attentive/ A young nigga with money will make niggas offended/ I ain't flashy I'm classy, but I ain't stupid either/ My sister's keeper, I'm loyal, it's all in my demeanor." -Car Confessions

Standing before a floor-length mirror in the living room, Noni palmed a brick of money as she rapped along with her favorite female rap artist, Young M.A.

Seated behind her at the dining room table was Asha and Lo-Lo, who were running their newly attained riches through an automated money counter. Also on the table were four credit cards associated with the phony business accounts. The plan had worked perfectly, for each card held a $25,000 credit line.

The 24-hour trap house had also been a huge success. With the quality of their products surpassing those of their competitors, it wasn't long before they reaching out to Perez for a re-up. And because Asha had paid their employees according to what was promised, not one staffer had a single complaint.

"Girl, can you really believe this?" Lo-Lo stared in disbelief at the stacks of money. "Just a month ago we was lower-class citizens. Now, we eating!"

"It just goes to show that the saying is true..." Asha smiled. "That a person can be your bum today, and your boss tomorrow."

After years of balancing on the tightrope of poverty, the tables had indeed turned. But Asha knew that with street-level success came jealous hearted weasels and insects of envy. So now, more than ever, they would have to be twice as deadly and cautious as serpents.

Interrupting Noni's mirror routine, Asha called her to come join them at the table. "Listen, I'm just as excited as y'all," she began, as her sister took a seat. "And I know it's gon' be hard, but we gotta stay focused. Because it's the only way we can avoid the same pitfalls of our predecessors."

Lo-Lo attentively leaned forward. "What you mean?"

"I'm saying, what better lessons than the ones from the legends who did it before us? Whether it was greed, cockiness, or whatever, we can look at their mistakes as like a map on where not to walk and what to be watchful of. And we know misplaced loyalty was where most 'em went wrong. So, we can't ever forget the first line of our oath."

"But what about Teer and Double-O?" Noni asked. "We shouldn't trust them like that, either?"

"Is not Griselda Blanco one of the most powerful women we know of?" Asha replied.

Both Lo-Lo and Noni nodded their heads.

"And was it not the man she let inside her heart the one who betrayed her? So that's exactly why I said we gotta be mindful of other people's mistakes. Now, I ain't saying we can't be fond of our friends. But what I am saying is that we gotta always be on guard. We can't put nothing past nobody. Because yo, we about to start seeing some serious paper. And if we ain't trying to be spending that shit on coffins or commissary, then we gotta move on some militant shit."

"Yeah, you right." Lo-Lo bobbed her head in agreement. "Cause it's been just us since forever. And we know Shawna gotta heart of gold. So outside of that, we can't lend our full trust to no one else. We gotta just stick to what we know."

"Exactly," Asha confirmed. "And I ain't saying we ain't gon' always play fair with our peoples. But we not gon' act as if we can't get bit. Because the moment you lower your guard, that's usually when it happens."

"Now come on," Asha rose from the table, "Let's put this shit up and go celebrate."

***

"A hundred-and-forty-six-thousand?" Shawna loudly whispered. She was expressing surprise at hearing their new net worth.

Asha grinningly nodded. "It's all coming together, love."

The girls' idea of celebrating was to visit Shawna and share with her the good news of their progressive steps. Because in spite of her troubled past or current placement, she was equally entitled to whatever they attained. For theirs was a love without conditions.

"Can you believe it's already been three months?" Lo-Lo smiled, laying a hand of encouragement on Shawna's arm. "Just think, three more and we'll officially be complete."

Touched by the latter part of Lo-Lo's statement, Shawna lowered her head in inner joy. It filled her insides with tingly feelings to know that she was loved to such a profound degree.

"I've made a lot shameful decisions in my life," Shawna looked at each of her sisters. "I could blame it on being scared, lonely, or simply feeling hopeless. But I won't. I can't. Because there's women who've had it worse than me, but still stood on certain morals. So there's no excuse. But I can say that the love y'all have shown me while at my lowest, for the second time, has made me realize that maybe there's more to my life than just pain and suffering. So I just want to say thank you for everything. But most importantly, thank you for believing in me when I didn't even believe in myself."

Surprised that Shawna wasn't in tears, they wordlessly rose to give her tight squeeze.

"So I'm saying," Noni eyed Shawna, as they sat back down. "Is your heart still in this Mob shit, or what?"

Shawna frowned in slight offense. "Of course. Y'all my sisters."

"Then you shouldn't have a problem remembering our oath," Noni tested her.

As Asha and Lo-Lo were watching her with hopeful thoughts, Shawna recited their friendship oath without hesitation.

"In my sister shall I trust... from my sister shall I learn. To her aid shall I rush... and for each other shall we burn."

Bearing a proud grin, Asha reached over to hold Shawna's hand.

"And who are you?" Noni continued.

"My sister's keeper," Shawna answered.

"And what's our crowning principle?"

"By L.O.V.E. we abide."

"And what's the definition of L.O.V.E.?"

Upon her giving the correct answer, Noni reached out to shake her hand. "B.F.M."

"For life!" Shawna solemnly replied.

As they sat around the table, sharing snacks and laughs, Lo-Lo looked over at Shawna with endearment.

"What?" Shawna smiled, curious to know what her sister was thinking.

"Nah, it's just, I'm so happy we found you. I can't even explain how I felt when I looked in the backseat that night and saw you. I know Asha always said the universe would bring you back to us, but after three years went by, I kind of started to lose faith. So for the four of us to be together right now just lets me know that this is really what's meant to be. And even though I know we gon' have obstacles ahead, there's no doubt in my mind that the time has come for us to spread our wings."

"I can definitely toast to that," Noni grabbed her bottle of water.

As the others followed suit, they bumped their bottles together and cheered in unison, "Butterfly Mafia!"

After taking a sip, Shawna stated, "Ain't it crazy how an ugly situation can blossom into something so beautiful?"

Bobbing their heads in agreement, their minds re-wound to how Butterfly Mafia initially came about.

Chapter 20

Flashback...

Amid the relentless chatter of several dozen girls, the twins and Lo-Lo sat at a dayroom table inside a juvenile detention center. Charged with multiple felonies, the most serious being drug trafficking, they were looking at possibly being incarcerated until the ages of twenty-one.

"My lawyer some bullshit," Lo-Lo stated in a hushed tone. "All he keep asking me is where we got the drugs from. Talking about if I tell the truth, it could help with my sentence."

Asha nodded. "Yeah, ours basically on the same shit. Not knowing that if we told the truth, they'd probably throw away the fucking key. So we just gon' have to ride it out and see what the magistrate do. And worst case scenario, we gotta do four years in this shit. But it's better than what they'd give us if they knew what really happened."

At the thought of what really happened, they turned their attention to Noni, who sat on top of the table with a murderous glare. This was a hostile environment where violence could erupt at given moment. A moment which Noni was eager to embrace.

Although it had been a year since the horrifying night of the home invasion, the twins sustained physical scars that served as constant reminders. Asha had a permanent mark beneath her left eye, and Noni had two false teeth, of which she was utterly self-conscious. Were it not for their collective craving for revenge, they would've likely went into a depressive seclusion, or on a suicidal rampage.

"Chow time! Chow time!" a woman's voice announced over a loudspeaker. "Everyone line up!"

As usual, the three girls lagged behind. They had no desire to develop friendships, so were careful to maintain their distance from the other inmates.

"Man, they serving this shit again?" Lo-Lo complained, as they returned to their table with trays of Beef Stroganoff.

"It ain't about the taste right now, love," Asha said, picking up her plastic spork. "Right now we just eating to live."

In the midst of them consuming a meal that a canine would decline; a staff member accompanied a new inmate into the pod.

Carrying a bedroll in one hand and a Styrofoam tray in the other, the girl had a head full of hair and a chocolate complexion. She kept her focus on the floor as she hurried to her room.

But no matter how low of a profile a person kept, there was always one out the bunch who thought it was cute to pick on those they perceived to be weak.

Trailed by two of her equally ignorant friends, a bully named Tessa headed toward the new girl's room. Tessa was the type to tease anyone with self-esteem lower than hers.

Asha turned to watch as Tessa entered the new girl's room without bothering to knock. Harboring a strong dislike for bullies, her heart started pounding.

When Tessa laughingly backpedaled out the girl's room a minute later, holding her Styrofoam tray, Asha went to stand up and Lo-Lo grabbed her arm. "That's not our fight, love. And besides, we gotta keep our nose clean before sentencing."

Asha considered her advice, then thought about how it felt to be in a position where you wished there was someone to intervene. But what finalized her decision was the envisioning of the new girl's innocent image.

"I can't stand by and watch that girl be mistreated," Asha said, gently removing Lo-Lo's hand from her arm. "Especially, when she ain't even did nothing. So I'm willing to accept whatever consequences that come behind my actions."

As Asha approached Tessa and her snickering crew, the pod got quieter than a church mouse. No one had ever been bold enough to confront the bully, and they were anxious to see how the scene played out.

Without a lick of fear in her eyes or voice, Asha stood before Tessa and calmly suggested, "Why don't you give that girl her food back. You didn't even eat yours, so you can't possibly be that hungry."

Tessa handed the tray to one of her minions and moved closer to Asha. "Why don't you mind your business, like you been doing. Before I go over there and take your shit, too."

Asha calmly stepped aside and extended her arm. "Be my guest."

Because the twins and Lo-Lo had stuck to themselves since their arrival, Tessa was unsure of what she was walking into. She took pride in being considered the "pod boss", and would hate to be demoted over something as simple as Beef Stroganoff. But knowing retreat at this point would make her look weak, her mind was nervously thinking of how to proceed.

But before she could conceive a solution, Noni impatiently banded her plaits into a ponytail and hopped up from the table. "Twin, we done talking!"

Going over to move Asha aside, Noni faced Tessa in a fighter's stance. "Either you gon' give that girl her tray back, or I'm putting your soft ass to sleep. Now, what's up?"

As nails of fear were being hammered into her throbbing heart, Tessa weakly replied, "It's whatever with me."

The pod watched in disbelief as Noni marched to Tessa's room and went in.

"Get your ass in in here!" Noni yelled from inside the cell.

As if her shoes were weighed down with lead, Tessa slowly trudged toward her room. Before disappearing inside, she glanced back at her crew for sign of support, but both girls quickly looked away.

"Close the door," Noni was heard saying.

Seconds after the door clicked shut, there was the sound of screeching shoes

With their feet anxious to run to the door and watch the fight, the girls in the pod groaned in disappointment when Asha warned them not to move. Because if one of the staff members happened to look at the camera and saw a bunch of people standing outside the door, then Noni would surely get caught.

To everyone's surprise, the screeching of shoes ended just as quickly as it begun.

Noni slid out the cell seconds later and gently shut the door. Turning to the dayroom, she put a finger to her lips and made a shushing sound. "She taking a nap."

Barely winded as she waved her hand in invitation, Noni told the girl holding the tray, "Come on, you next," then went to her cell.

Her eyes wide, she stood frozen in fear like a deer in headlights.

"Is you coming, or what?" Noni stuck her head out the girl's room.

"Th-th-this shit ain't even that serious," she nervously stuttered before returning the tray to its rightful owner.

As Noni was being regarded with starstruck stares, Asha went to introduce herself to the new girl. When she entered her room after softly knocking, she was caught off guard by what she witnessed.

Curled up on the bed in a fetal position, the girl's body was shivering as is she was lying outside in the middle of winter.

Familiar with the effects of drug withdrawal, Asha waved to Lo-Lo for assistance.

"She on heroin," Lo-Lo easily concluded, as she peered into the room. There had been a number of nights when her own mother had shivered in the exact same manner.

She just a baby, Asha shook her head in sadness at the pitiful sight. With Lo-Lo's help, she managed to wrap the girl in several blankets.

As they were on the verge of leaving the room, the girl looked up at Asha with a sad eyes that grabbed her by the heart and wouldn't let go. For in the girl's eyes was a reflection of pain that went beyond her current condition. This was someone who'd been the victim of traumatic experiences.

Able to understand and relate, Asha was compelled to cradle the girl in her arms. "I'm here, love," she comforted, gently rocking. "And I'm not gon' let you go through this alone."

When Noni appeared in the doorway and took in the touching scene, her expression softened in sympathy. And she knew in that moment that her sister made the right call in choosing to intervene.

Over the next week, they faithfully sat by the girl's bedside. They dried her tears when she cried for a fix; cleaned her vomit when her stomach refused food; and bathed her when she had bowel movements beyond her control. With patience, they nurtured the girl back to her original self.

Shy by nature, the girl, Shawna, revealed that she was 15-years-old and all alone. Her mother had died from an overdose, and her granny was the embodiment of evil. She had once been befriended by an older girl named Puma, who saved her from an ongoing case of sexual abuse. But after her savior was slaughtered by merciless vultures, she was once again left to fend for herself. With no other means of coping with the pain, she sought comfort in the arms of the killer that murdered her mother; secretly hoping that one day maybe she'd encounter the same fate.

Her testimony touched each girl on a different level. Asha could relate to being young and motherless. Lo-Lo understood what it was like to lose a parent to drug abuse. And Noni personally knew how it felt to be sexually violated. So despite Shawna being younger in age and a complete stranger, they developed a close-knit bond with her that was surely brought about by the universe. And because they were pure hearted young ladies, with an excellent judge of character, they would embrace Shawna as if she was their biological sister.

The four were gathered at the dayroom table one day, having lunch, when Shawna stopped eating and quietly spoke, "The girl Puma I told y'all about was the only person to ever show me love. And I can remember telling her that I didn't think I'd ever meet nobody else who would care about me. But now I realize I was wrong. Because I don't know how I could've got through my sickness without y'all being there. So I just want to say how grateful I am for the love and support. Which for me is something uncommon."

As their bond with Shawna grew stronger by the day, she was soon like a natural part of the group. With her innocent demeanor, wild bush of hair, and chubby chocolate cheeks, she was the younger sister they never had but always wanted.

And Shawna was just as endeared by each of their characters. Lo-Lo was the cool white girl, who was very pretty and fiercely loyal. Asha was the mother figure. And Noni was the overprotective enforcer who had a warm heart beneath her cold exterior.

No longer having a bully in the pod, as Tessa had moved after being publicly exposed, the atmosphere was mostly clear of tension. There were still petty quarrels on occasion but gone were the days of verbal abuse and extortion. Even the TV remote was now being freely passed around.

It was on a Sunday morning, when Lo-Lo was flicking through the channels. "Hold up, go back!" Shawna had blurted out.

Upon Lo-Lo doing so, Shawna smiled at the sight of a butterfly that floated through the forest.

Asha observed her with an inquisitive look, which Shawna noticed.

"Seeing that butterfly reminded me of something Puma once told me," Shawna said in fondness of the memory.

Shortly before Puma's untimely death, she had explained to Shawna that she could do anything she set her mind to. Being an underdog just meant you had to walk a little farther and fight a little harder. But it was the final part of Puma's statement that had stuck with Shawna. "I may not be around to see it, but one day you gon' blossom into a beautiful butterfly."

Later that day, as they were lounging in Lo-Lo's room, Asha could tell that Shawna had something on her mind. "What you over there thinking about, love?"

Amazed by her friend's perceptiveness, Shawna said she was wondering if they could give themselves a name.

"Like what?" Asha genuinely inquired.

"I don't know," Shawna giggled. "But something that stands out and represents the four of us."

Intrigued by the idea, the girls began blurting out all sorts of names for a girl gang.

In memory of Puma, Shawna's only request was that the name have something to do with a butterfly.

"A butterfly does have four wings," Lo-Lo pointed out. And it is four of us."

"And one day we gon' take over the city on some mob shit!" Noni chimed in.

Lo-Lo looked at Noni. "Girl, what the mob gotta do with a butterfly?"

Blocking out their exited chatter, Asha was pondering over Shawna's request, when a bulb of enlightenment blinked on in her mind. Right now they were just four juvenile girls who spun in a cocoon of afflictions. But their will to survive would one day enable them to shed the distressing encasement and evolve into what they were destined to be. Hence, the struggle could be likened to the caterpillar stage, and to endure was to evolve into beautiful butterflies.

"Aye, I think I got it," Asha said, bearing a broad smile as she knowingly bobbed her head.

The chatter instantly ceased as they turned to face her in anticipation. "What?"

"We could call ourselves..." Asha purposely paused to heighten the suspense, "Butterfly Mafia."

Chapter 21

Flint, Michigan...

Asha parked a gray Nissan Altima in front of the building where the girl, D'Aura lived. Unlike most people who were poor in principles, Asha took pride in upholding her promises.

Ascending the building's front porch, she pressed D'Aura's buzzer and was let in seconds later.

With her daughter peeking around her leg, D'Aura was standing in the doorway of her apartment as Asha came down the hall.

"Hi, pretty girl!" Asha waved to the 5-year-old, who burst out in a fit of giggles.

Inside the apartment, the two women hugged before taking a seat on the sofa.

"I ain't even gon' perp," D'Aura admitted, "I doubted you, girl. I mean, I know what you did and said last time, but I never expected to hear from you again. I've been lied to and let down by family members. But the fact that you sitting here right now says a whole lot about your character. So regardless of where we go from here, I'll have respect for you for the rest of my life."

Asha leaned over to hug her again. "Thank you, love, I appreciate that. But I'm only doing what real women supposed to. 'Cause we all we got, you hear me? So whenever we in a position to help somebody who from the same struggle, we obligated to step in. And trust me, the universe ain't rewarding that selfish shit."

Impressed by the depth of Asha's perspective, D'Aura smiled, "You sure you only twenty? Because it's women my age who ain't thinking like that."

At 25-years-old, D'Aura had overcame her fair share of hurdles and hardships. Having grown up without a father figure, or a mother who could stay out of jail, D'Aura was doing the best she could in her journey through life. She was desperate to improve her situation, but it seemed so hard to get ahead when you've been clawing for survival since childhood.

But as a woman who wasn't weakened by envy, it gave her a sense of strength to see someone like her standing firm against the winds of adversity. So in spite of her struggling to make ends meet, she was proud of Asha, who was a source of inspiration.

"One thing you gotta remember is this," Asha reasoned, "Just like every man wasn't cut out to be a king, neither can every woman carry herself like a queen. It's only a few of us, love. And that's why I be stressing the importance of looking out for each other. When we first met, I didn't expect to embrace you. But I felt your energy, and I had no choice but to respond accordingly. And all I ask for in return is that you're ever in the position, do the same for someone else."

With that said, Asha reached in her purse and pulled out an envelope, which she handed to D'Aura. "This should be enough to fill the fridge, the gas tank, and whatever else you can think of."

When D'Aura peered inside the envelope, her eyes widened at what appeared to be all hundred-dollar bills. "Oh, my god, girl, how much is this?"

Smiling at what she sensed was a genuinely appreciative reaction, Asha answered, "Five thousand."

Her mouth hung open, but D'Aura was speechless. Not one other person on earth had ever given her such a much needed and generous gift.

Slowly shaking her head in amazement as she continued to stare at the money, D'Aura shrugged, "I don't even know what to say right now. Because it's like, what words could possibly measure up to something like this?"

She turned to face Asha and there were tears in her eyes. "I work hard for every dime I get. And it's never enough. I love my little girl with every bone in my body, but my nos outweigh my yesses". And I ain't never blamed nobody for my struggles, but, girl, sometimes this shit be feeling like it's too much. I be emotionally drained. And the only thing that keeps me going is knowing my baby needs me."

Concerned by her mother's tears, the little girl, Polaris, came over to lay a chubby hand on D'Aura's face. "Mama, why you cry?"

D'Aura smiled at her in affection. "I'm okay, baby. These are tears of joy. Mama not sad. And if you promise to be a good girl, I gotta special surprise for you."

"Oooh!" her big brown eyes brightened with excitement. "I promise, mama. I promise."

"Alright, well, I need you to go play with your toys while I finish talking, okay?"

"Okay, mama?" Polaris replied before obediently running off.

As the little girl resumed playing with her Barbie dolls, Asha regretted not bringing along more money. The exchange between mother and daughter touched her in a profound way. And she couldn't help but wish that her own mother would've cherished her and Noni on a similar scale.

Asha glanced at her watch. "Listen, I don't have time to get into it right now, but there's some stuff I want to talk to you about. I gotta shoot out of town for two weeks, but I definitely need to link up with you when I get back."

"Is everything cool?" D'Aura asked in concern.

"Of course," Asha assured her. "I just want us to sit down and talk. Listen, I don't mind feeding you, love. But because I see the potential beneath the pain, I'd rather give you the push you need so you can feed yourself."

There was no longer any amount of doubt in D'Aura's mind that Asha was a woman of her word. In fact, she'd wager every penny in Polaris' piggy bank that Asha would eventually be erected into a figure of empowerment. And for that reason, she was willing to follow the counsel of a woman who was five years her junior.

Walking Asha to the door, D'Aura reiterated how grateful she was for the money. "I can catch up on my bills, get my baby some clothes, and even get some new tires for my car."

Screwing her face up in distaste, Asha shook her head, "Girl, don't waste your money like that. If anything, you should take that mu'fucka to the nearest scarp yard and see what they'll give you for it."

D'Aura laughed, "I wish I could. Because Lord knows I be so embarrassed by how noisy that thing is. But right now it's what's getting me back and forth to work."

After giving Asha a loving hug, D'Aura encouraged her daughter to say bye.

To both women's surprise, Polaris came from behind her mother and held out her little arms. She wanted a hug, too.

As Asha inhaled her childlike scent, she thought she would break down in tears right there in the doorway. There was something about a child's affection you just couldn't explain.

Thanking Polaris for the big hug, Asha told D'Aura she'd be in touch and turned to leave.

When D'Aura closed the door and locked it, she was startled by a sharp knock.

Peering through the peephole, she quickly unlocked and opened the door in concern. "Is everything okay?"

Asha handed her a set of car keys. "It's a gray Nissan Altima outside. It got brand-new tires, it ain't noisy... and it's yours."

As D'Aura's jaw dropped in shock, Asha laughingly backpedaled down the hallway. "Girl, I gotta go. But I'ma call you soon as I get back. Now pick your jaw up and go check out your new ride."

Outside, Asha approached an SUV and climbed into its backseat. Up front was Lo-Lo and the Mexican girl, Angel.

"Girl, you glowing like a mu'fucka," Lo-Lo smiled, as she took in Asha's joyful radiance.

"Like, literally," Angel chimed in.

Slowly shaking her head, Asha beamed. "Yo, I swear it ain't a better feeling in the world than looking out for somebody who really in need. And if I could put that feeling in a bottle and sell it, I'd be a billionaire in no time."

As Lo-Lo drove off, Angel was further intrigued by the girl in the backseat. It was no secret that Asha was the matriarch. But the way she managed to balance the scales of kindness and cruelty was nothing short of amazing. So while Angel was physically drawn to Noni, she mentally in love with her twin sister.

"So how you feeling about bringing D'Aura on board?" Lo-Lo inquired, as she drove them to the airport. Knowing Asha like the back of her hand, Lo-Lo knew she had already entertained the idea.

"I think she'd make a good addition," Asha admitted. "But I'll definitely be able to make a decision when we get back."

Unbeknownst to D'Aura, the gifts were more than just a charitable act. They were also a means for Asha to see her character in its true form. The 20-year-old may have had a generous heart, but she also had a mind that was exceptionally shrewd.

Chapter 22

"You know you want to text her back," Double-O told Noni, as she weaved through traffic in the GTO. "I see how you keep looking at your phone."

"Nah, I'm good," she shook her head. "Because if she was so worried about me, then she should've took me with her."

"Girl, you hear how you sound?" CJ teased from the backseat. "Like a grown ass spoiled baby."

"Alright, nigga," Noni jokingly warned, "I done whooped niggas for much less."

Although it had only been two months since the day Noni had him ghostride his mountain bike, CJ's authentic energy enabled him to fit right in. And the same could be said for Double-O, whom Noni had bonded with on a brotherly level.

Noni turned down the block on which their new trap house was located. With it bearing the same setup as the former spot, she parked across the street from the light-blue building and killed the lights.

In the backseat, CJ lifted a blanket to uncover an AR-15 assault rifle. Modified to fully auto, he checked to make sure there was a round in the chamber and lowered his window midway.

After careful deliberation, Asha had thought of a way to stay a step ahead of authorities. Her reasoning was why run the risk of a raid, when they could simply change locations every thirty days. So by the time the cops caught wind of the excessive traffic, they'd already be serving out of a different building. And their products were potent enough to where their customers would follow them to the end of the earth.

Having waited until there was a break in traffic, Teer emerged from the downstairs apartment and hurried around to the side of the building. Seconds later a small bag was tossed out of the upstairs window.

"What's this?" Noni asked, as Teer came up to the car and gave her the bag.

"Eighty-three hundred, and some change."

At the rate they were rowing, Noni knew her team would soon be sailing on the waters of wealth.

"So, what y'all about to get into?" Teer inquired, cautiously scanning both ends of the street.

"Shit, I don't know what these niggas about to do," Noni stroked her chin as if she had a full beard. "But I'm about to fuck something. I'm on some super horny shit."

"Alright, well, I'ma let you get to it," Teer chuckled, reaching inside the car to shake each of their hands. "I'll see y'all tomorrow. And stay alert."

After watching him safely reenter the apartment, Noni flicked the lights and pulled off.

"I'm saying, though, Noni," CJ spoke up, "You just made that shit sound like you the only one who got pussy on deck."

"That certainly wasn't my intention. So, I apologize if I hurt your little fragile ass feelings."

CJ grinned. "Aw, I see you got jokes, huh?"

In a competitive mood, CJ dug a Frank from his pocket and held it up. "Shit, I gotta dollar to say we can let Double-O pick any bitch in the club, and she'll come with me before she go with you."

Banging her fist on the wheel, Noni squealed in excitement at the challenge. "Not only do I call," she eagerly dug in her pocket, "But I raise you four hundred."

When they delegated Double-O to be the holder of the pot, he put his hands up in refusal. "I don't want no parts of that. Because y'all know Asha said to keep a low profile while she gone."

Noni eyed him with a sour taste in her mouth. "Nigga, is Asha your mama? Because she damn sure ain't mine!"

"Man, that ain't even got nothing to do w—"

"Is y'all fucking, or something?"

"Come on, Noni..."

"Nah, I'm saying, you sitting here acting like you ain't a grown ass man. Talking about what Asha said."

Double-O glared at her growled, "I've been a man since I was twelve."

"Well, act like it, then, got-dammit."

CJ leaned up from the backseat and smiled. "Noni, you don't see what's going on? This hating ass nigga done seen me in action with them hoes. And he just trying to stop me from taking your money."

"But it's cool, though," CJ added with a slight shrug, "Cause I don't want Asha to come back and find out I done took her sister up top, anyway."

"Aw, nigga!" Noni smiled, using her elbow to nudge him out of her space. "Now, you the one with jokes."

"But nah, for real, bro," CJ looked at Double-O, "Tell her how I could've been a pimp if I hadn't of started stealing cars."

Double-O flashed an amused smile, "I mean, I've seen you with a few girls. But, bro, I don't know about all that pimp shit."

CJ sat back in his seat. "Yeah, Noni, we might need to drop this hating ass nigga off and do our own thing."

Noni laughed, "Now you mad 'cause he ain't vouching for that bullshit. Nigga, if anything, I should drop your fake Pimpin Ken ass off."

As the car was idling at a red light, Noni and Double-O glanced at each other. She lifted her head in acknowledgment, and he returned the gesture. She flinched at him, and he flinched back at her. Then, when she smiled in affection, he genuinely followed suit. And just like that the love was renewed and the quarrel forgotten.

They were coming up Seven Mile, when Noni's attention was drawn to the crowded lot of a liquor store.

"Look like that bet might still be on," she looked back at CJ, flicking her left-turn signal. "And we ain't even gotta go to the club."

Whipping into the crowded parking lot, where a number of men and women were loudly loitering, Noni squeezed among a variety of vehicles and threw the car in park.

"This your last chance to stand down," she warned CJ, with her hand on the door handle.

"Likewise," he cockily replied.

"Alright, nigga, don't say I didn't warn you."

Planted next to a Silverado across the parking lot, Pierre was talking to a shapely built woman, when he saw Noni exit her car. "Aye, hold up right quick," he said before walking off.

When Noni sensed someone coming towards her and looked back, Pierre threw up his hands and smiled, "What's up with the Mob?"

"What's good, lil' bruh?" she greeted, giving him a handshake and hug.

"Damn, girl, what you been up to?" he inquired, curiously peering over her shoulder at Double-O and CJ. "I ain't seen you around in a minute."

Pinching her nose at the unpleasant odor coming from Pierre's energy, Noni casually scanned her surroundings and replied, "I been chilling. But what's up with you? What you doing way over here?"

He nudged his head in the direction of the truck, "I'm with my big homie. We about to go to the club and fuck it up, you feel me."

"Yeah, that's what's up," she nodded, then shot Double-O a look that made him get on point.

Unconsciously fiddling with his hands in nervousness, Pierre awkwardly smiled. "You know, it's crazy, 'cause I was just telling the big homie about you. How you be on some turnt shit. And he was saying how he wanted to meet you."

Before she could inquire about his "big homie's" identity, he unfolded himself from the driver seat of the Silverado.

When Smurf came around the pickup, sporting a diamond chain and designer jeans, Double-O eyed him in mild surprise. For Smurf had once been a member of his former crew.

CJ, however, was heated by his presence, as Smurf was the same selfish man who had found a life jacket when their ship was sinking, but left him to drown.

Unsure of where him and Double-O stood, Smurf just lifted his head in acknowledgment. "What's good, bro? When you touch down?"

"A few months ago," he answered, making no effort to physically embrace him. Because if he had truly left a comrade to starve, then Double-O had no desire to revive their friendship. Disloyalty was a violation for which there was no forgiveness.

"Yeah, well, we definitely need to link up," Smurf suggested, "'Cause I ain't forgot about everything you and King did for a nigga. We was the Few Against Many, remember?"

CJ lost it at that point. "Nigga, how you gon' stand here and holler that F.A.M. shit, when soon as shit hit the fan, you left a nigga for dead!"

"Because you ain't no hustler!" Smurf barked back. "You a fucking car thief, nigga. And that ain't what I'm into. So how the fuck was I supposed to feed you?"

Disappointed in Smurf's response, Double-O spoke up, "I see you gotta bad memory, my baby."

Smurf frowned in confusion. "And how is that?"

156

"Because clearly you forgot it was a certain semi-truck that put us in the game."

It took only a split second for Smurf to make the connection. And though his pride wouldn't allow him to verbally admit it, it was indeed because of CJ they were fed their first taste of fortune and fame.

Nearly five years ago, Double-O and his best friend, King, had been informed about a low-key gambling spot in the basement of a dance club. But with armed security guards who were licensed to kill, and had done so in the past, it would require the element of surprise for them to avoid a botched robbery.

One of the coldest car thieves across the continent, it was CJ who would use a screwdriver and channel locks to steal a semi-truck, which they drove through a front window of the club. Making off with close to a hundred grand, Double-O and his team had entered the drug game on a grand scale.

As Smurf offered a lame excuse on behalf of his disloyal actions, Noni instinctively keyed in on a dark colored Charger that entered the parking lot. Observing the car out the corner of her eye, its tinted windows prevented her from seeing inside. But when she glanced at Pierre, who quickly averted her gaze, her heartbeat quickened in alarm.

Removing the micro Hellcat from the small of her back, she saw a hooded figure creeping towards them in a crouched position. And jutting from the butt of his gun was a clip the length of a ruler.

Without a clear shot, Noni pointed her gun skywards and fired. But as the crowd fearfully scattered in different directions, she lost sight of the gunman.

With his arm extended as he got within shooting distance, the gunman carefully aimed at Noni's back. Having no time to react, she felt his presence behind her and knew she'd been caught slipping.

At the thunderous discharge of a large-caliber firearm, the gunman spun around from a round that ripped through his right shoulder. But before Double-O could finish him off, the gunman blindly returned fire and managed to make it back to the getaway car.

Her heart still pounding, Noni looked over her shoulder at Double-O with an look that expressed her deepest gratitude; for he had literally just saved her life. And it was in that moment when she knew they would be friends forever.

As the Charger exited the parking lot with a loud squeal, CJ ran out into the street with the AR-15 and opened fire, shattering the back windshield before the car turned a corner and disappeared.

When Noni pulled alongside CJ and slammed on the brakes, Double-O opened his door and yelled, "Get in!"

As they sped off down a side street, neither of the three paid attention to the pearl-white Mercedes Benz truck, which had been present for majority of the ordeal.

Behind its tinted windows were the vengeful sisters, Mecca and Unique. Having went against their initial decision, they had agreed to let Smurf arrange the murders of the two women he claimed to be responsible for their cousin's deaths. Their only condition was that they be present to witness it.

"Get Hotrod on the phone," Mecca spat in disgust, bringing the engine to life. "Because I can go to the circus if I want to see some clown shit."

Also a native of Flint, Michigan, Hotrod was a young livewire who thrived on chaos. And for a few grand he'd murder a whole household.

When he answered after several rings, Unique skipped the pleasantries and asked him if he wanted to make some money.

"Hell yeah!" Hotrod replied, recalling how handsomely they'd paid him in the past.

"Alright, well go put yourself up till we get there. Because trust me, we gon' make this one well worth it."

While en route to their hometown, the sisters expressed their surprise at seeing Double-O. It was due solely to his imprisonment that he had escaped their wrath in the past. But this time they would ensure he wasn't so lucky. And with his actions at the liquor store reminding them of how dangerous he was, they would encourage Hotrod to recruit an accomplice who was equally experienced.

With their bank accounts containing close to seven figures, the sisters would pay whatever it took to stop Double-O and the twins from breathing.

Chapter 23

It was a sunny afternoon in California, when a 757 Boeing landed at LAX airport. Among the first group of passengers to exit the plane were Asha, Lo-Lo, and Angel. Donning dark shades, and travelling with only carry-on luggage, they were on the west coast for business and pleasure, but mainly business.

A driver and his discreetly armed copilot were standing before a Private Class Sprinter, with their hands clasped behind their backs.

"Are you with First Class Customs?" Lo-Lo inquired of the driver.

"We are," he answered with a single nod. "And you must be Ms. Tannerhill."

Wearing the same disguise as she had on the day she visited the banks, Lo-Lo removed her phony ID for verification.

After a careful inspection, the driver extended his hand and introduced himself as Marty Bridges. "And this is my partner and copilot, Chris Henson."

Following a round of introductory handshakes, the copilot activated the power sliding door and advised the women to watch their step.

"This mu'fucka like a small condo," Lo-Lo commented, as they settled in leather swivel seats. Equipped with state-of-the-art appliances and cabinetry, the Sprinter had everything from a miniature bathroom to Apple TV.

"Will we be sticking to the itinerary, Ms. Tannerhill?" the copilot turned to question. Prior to their arrival at the airport, the two employees were provided with an itinerary that listed their customer's prearranged destinations.

160

Enjoying the tone of respect in which she was addressed, Lo-Lo gave an affirmative nod. "We will, Chris."

As they were driven through the city of Los Angeles, the girls were all smiles while taking in the palm trees and other passing scenery. This was Asha and Lo-Lo's first time out of Michigan, and their level of excitement was beyond description. They couldn't wait to one day return with Noni and Shawna, a time when it would be strictly pleasure.

Upon reaching their first destination, it felt like they had just rolled into a different realm of the universe. For this was a place Asha and Lo-Lo had dreamed of attending since adolescence, Rodeo Drive. A two-mile strip that stretched from Los Angeles to Beverly Hills, it was known as one of the most expensive streets in the world.

The copilot lowered the privacy partition. "We'll be parked right here whenever you're finished."

Lo-Lo handed him two crisp bills. "Y'all might want to take a three hour lunch break."

Exiting the sprinter, the girls gawked at the long line of boutiques with starry-eyes.

"Girl, we here!" Lo-Lo squealed, squeezing Asha's arm in utter delight.

While she was just as excited, Asha reminded Lo-Lo on the importance of displaying dignified demeanors. They were financing this adventure in a fraudulent manner, and to appear overly excited could arouse unwanted suspicion.

After leisurely browsing through a number of stores, Lo-Lo settled on a leather bomber, double-denim jeans and four-inch heels. Asha went for a more casual approach, with a hooded tracksuit and pink Dior sneakers.

Lo-Lo's heart was galloping faster than a horse in full stride as she approached the counter. She knew the credit cards were activated, as she used them to purchase the plane tickets and chauffer service, but this would be her first time using one in person.

Once the purchase was successfully completed, she accepted the card and receipt with a smile of relief. "Thank you, ma'am, and you have a nice day."

When they stepped outside, Angel teased her, "Tell me why I saw your heart beating through your shirt."

"And tell me why I heard that mu'fucka hammering like a construction crew," Asha laughingly chimed in.

"Yeah, well, let me see how calm y'all would be if it was you stepping up to that counter."

Angel held out her hand.

Lo-Lo shot her a sideways glance. "Girl, if you don't cut the games. You know you don't look like shit like a white woman named Jessica Tannerhill."

"My complexion don't, but my confidence do," Angel said, as they were on the verge of entering Louis Vuitton. "Now gimme one of them cards and let me show you how a real Mexican get down."

Because Angel would soon be playing a role that required her to fit the image of a boss, she had to shop for a more expensive outfit than the Lo-Lo and Asha's. Picking out a cashmere peacoat, a lovely marigold turtleneck, and knee-high boots with the pointed toe. She would definitely look the part of a woman who was about her business.

Approaching the counter as if she was indeed Jessica Tannerhill, Angel handed the male employee a PNC credit card and smiled. "Am I wrong for leaving my husband in the car for all this time?"

"Honey, this is what we do," he flamboyantly replied. "So he'll just have to understand."

Upon exiting the store, Angel turned to Lo-Lo in triumph. "My bro taught me long ago that even if you dead wrong, you still gotta play it like you all the way in the right. Because energy a muthafucka."

Their next stop was at Tiffany's, where they topped off Angel's outfit with a ring that implied she was married to a millionaire.

When they returned to the Sprinter with all their bags, the driver jokingly stated, "You sure you don't need us to take another lunch break?"

After stopping for pizza at a renowned restaurant called Big Mamas, which specialized in supersized pizzas, they were driven to a hotel near the downtown area.

"Well, fellas, it's been real," Lo-Lo said, reaching up front to shake their hands. "But I'm afraid our time has come to an end."

They thanked her in genuine gratitude when she rewarded them with a $500 tip. They watched the Sprinter exit the parking lot before marching down the street to a different hotel. One that was less conspicuous, and accepted cash.

Inside a small, shabby room with one bed, they transferred hygienic and other personal items from their carry-on's to their shopping bags. They looked around as if pondering over where to hide the luggage, then thought better of it upon remembering it was knockoff. And besides, they had no plans on returning to Michigan with the bags anyway.

"So you really believe we can pull this off in a week?" Angel asked Asha, as they waited for the arrival of their Uber.

"I do," she nodded. "Because I believe in the power of greed. And I've personally seen it override common sense and caution. So we just gotta make sure we play our parts, and there's no doubt in my mind that everything else gon' fall in place."

Lo-Lo bobbed her head in agreement. Because not only did she also believe in the power of greed, but she believed in the power of Asha's brain. The girl had a clever mind that had kept them afloat since she could remember. So when the cards were dealt and the chips were pushed, Lo-Lo would bet big on Asha every single time.

Their Uber arrived in the form of a four-door Ford Taurus.

Placing their shopping bags in the trunk, they piled in the backseat and Lo-Lo gave the driver the name and address of a rental car agency.

As they rode through traffic, Lo-Lo glanced at Asha and noticed her gazing out the window in deep thought. Knowing she was thinking about Noni, Lo-Lo reached out to squeeze her hand in comfort, to which Asha responded with an appreciative smile.

Arriving at a rental agency that dealt only in exotics, Lo-Lo went inside to pick up the keys to a reserved SUV.

When Lo-Lo whipped a Bentley Bentayga next to the Taurus and lowered her window, Angel let out a shriek of excitement.

Hurriedly hauling their bags from the car to the truck, Asha and Angel hopped in and Lo-Lo sped out the parking lot.

"Bitch, we in a Bentley truck!" Angel exclaimed, reaching up front to grip Asha's shoulder.

Asha winced at the B word. And though she hated to dampen Angel's lively mood, this was something she had to immediately address.

"Don't take this offensive, love," she turned to face Angel, "But don't ever refer to me as a bitch."

"My bad, girl, I'm sorry. But you know I didn't mean no harm."

"And that's why I'm not upset. But I ain't no female dog, and I ain't conforming to that disrespectful ass word. Because if a person ain't gon' refer to they mama or granny as a bitch, then they ain't gon' refer to me as one either."

"I mean, and think about it," Lo-Lo chimed in, "Can't no woman possibly consider herself a queen but allow herself or no one else to call her a bitch. Because the two words can't even fit in the same category. So even though a lot of women have accepted it, the Mob ain't going. And we'll burn in Hell over something as simple as a word."

Asha raised the four fingers of her hand and stamped, "And that's on all four wings of Butterfly Mafia!"

Angel could only nod to herself in understanding and respect. Because it was true, women had been verbally assaulted with the derogatory term for so long, that a great number had kneeled in submission. But just because men have fell short of the glory of kings, that doesn't mean a woman shouldn't be treated in accordance to the queen she is. Sadly, it's now on the woman to assume control of the throne.

"Snap out of it," Asha smiled, as she took in the contemplative look on Angel's face. "That was just some food for thought. You can digest it later."

"Nah, girl, that was some real shit y'all said. Because a reference that women once found repulsive has now been adopted into their own vocabulary. Which, when you really think about it, is some psychologically deep shit."

Asha and Lo-Lo burst out in laughter.

"What?" Angel asked in confusion of their sudden outburst.

Lo-Lo eyed her through the rearview. "Girl, you just went ham! Got to using all them big ass words and shit. We call ourselves dropping a few jewels on you, and you took it to whole nother level."

With their shared laughter restoring the former vibe, the girls moved on to different, and less sensitive subjects.

When they arrived in Malibu, GPS led them to the circular driveway of a miniature mansion. At $2,500 a night, the Air BNB was there's for a week.

Lowering their bags to the foyer's floor, the girls took a moment to admire the interior design of a seven-figure home. They had previewed the property through online pictures, but there was no comparison to seeing it in person.

After a leisure tour of its downstairs area and the modernized kitchen, they removed their shoes before climbing a suspended French Oak staircase.

Lo-Lo covered her mouth in awe at the sight of the Master Suite bedroom, where across from a Japanese soaking tub was a glass shower large enough to host an event.

"Look," Angel directed their attention to the vaulted ceiling, where a retractable sky light gave view to the overhead stars.

Venturing out onto a patio, Lo-Lo was ready to remove her clothes as she peered down at the in-ground pool with an Infinity edge.

"One day we gon' live like this," Asha mumbled to no one in particular. Her belief was that nearly anything in life was attainable. It simply boiled down to the amount of ambition in a person's possession.

Later that night, as they were lounging in the living room area, Lo-Lo noticed Asha kept her checking her phone. "Call her, love," she urged, knowing Asha was worried about Noni.

Asha stubbornly shook her head, "I've already texted her three times, Lo. I can't keep babying that girl. Especially when I know she just upset about me not bringing her with me. But I told her this ain't no vacation, this business."

"Yeah, but you know how Noni is. She spoiled and over-protective. And I hate to say it, but it's partly your fault. Because you've been spoiling that girl her whole life. So she doesn't understand the word "no" coming from her twin."

Although Lo-Lo made clear sense, Asha wasn't budging. She was just as stubborn as her twin sister.

But as the night progressed and Noni still didn't reach out, Asha went from irritated to angry. Her and Noni both had iPhones, so she knew her sister had read the texts.

Snatching the covers over her head, she couldn't believe Noni was being so childish as to purposely not reply.

Chapter 24

"Alright, I'ma get up with y'all tomorrow," Noni said to Double-O and CJ, as she pulled into to their apartment complex.

"You sure you don't want me to roll with you," Double-O asked, as he gave her a handshake.

"Nigga, I'm 'bout to get some pussy," Noni crudely remarked. "What, your lil' freaky ass trying to watch, or something?"

"Hell nah," Double-O smirked. "I'm just trying to make sure you safe."

Noni withdrew the Hellcat from her waistband and held it up. "This bitch hold thirty. If that ain't enough to keep me safe, then I don't know what is."

As Noni was driving out of the complex, she glanced at her rearview and saw Double-O staring after the car with a strange look on his face. She considered turning around but went against her better judgement and kept going.

Across town, Noni parked several houses down from a particular house and sent a short text, that said she outside.

Minutes later, a brown skin woman came out the house and hurried towards the car. She was wearing Adidas leggings and a tank top that barely contained her bouncing breasts.

"Damn, girl," Noni said, as the woman arranged her voluptuous frame inside the car. "You make me want to fuck you right here in the front seat."

The woman laughed before looking back at the house. "Gon' and pull off before his nosy ass get to peeking out the window."

When they paused at a stop sign on the corner, Noni grabbed the woman by the back of her neck and drew her in for a passionate kiss.

"Mmm," she moaned into Noni's mouth, as their tongues intertwined in a sensual dance.

The kiss was interrupted by the blaring of a horn behind them.

"Oh shit!" Noni laughingly pulled off.

"Mmph," the woman eyed Noni with a lustfully. "I ain't been kissed like that in a minute. Now, I'm just hoping you can fuck me better than my man."

In reply, Noni took the woman's hand and put it on her crouch.

When the woman's eyes widened in surprise, Noni was pleased to inform her, "This mu'fucka eight inches long, thick as shit, and it don't never go soft."

"Noni, watch out!" the woman screamed, as a small child ran out into the street.

Her heart lunged against her chest as she slammed on the brakes.

When the little boy rose up, he was holding a soccer ball.

Exhaling in relief, Noni turned to address her companion and felt her world stop moving, for the woman was staring past her with a look of frozen terror.

Upon dreadfully turning to stare at the person standing on the other side of her car window, Noni couldn't believe her eyes.

And before she could reach for her weapon, Double-O aligned an assault rifle with her head and opened fire.

To Be Continued...

(The Greatest Gift)

I'll strive to describe something beautiful to behold, yet impossible to define... Divine! the descriptive word that arrived in my mind when I thought of how lovely this gift was designed.

For it listens, it strengthens, and when we take it for granted it grants us forgiveness... with its primary mission to lend us assistance and enrich our existence.

I've witnessed it empower the powerless and provide the poor with a spirit of richness... I've witnessed it reassemble broken hearts and cure the dejected of emotional sickness.

This gift is as sacred as marriage, the reason for which it was meant to be cherished... look how it travels the globe, spilling pearls of compassion from its merciful carriage.

As children we loved to envelop ourselves in its bountiful blanket of warmth and affection... an indestructible force that derived from a source who connects with all shapes and complexions.

Without its remarkable presence this planet couldn't breed not one single Queen... it has a prevailing effect that can soften a savage and upgrade his thinking to that of a King.

So you may want to overprotect it as if you're protecting your own precious cub... and in case you were curious, this gift goes by the name of... A Woman's Love!

Yours truly,
Fumiya Payne.

Lock Down Publications and Ca$h Presents
Assisted Publishing Packages

BASIC PACKAGE	UPGRADED PACKAGE
$499	$800
Editing	Typing
Cover Design	Editing
Formatting	Cover Design
	Formatting
ADVANCE PACKAGE	**LDP SUPREME PACKAGE**
$1,200	$1,500
Typing	Typing
Editing	Editing
Cover Design	Cover Design
Formatting	Formatting
Copyright registration	Copyright registration
Proofreading	Proofreading
Upload book to Amazon	Set up Amazon account
	Upload book to Amazon
	Advertise on LDP, Amazon and Facebook Page

***Other services available upon request.
Additional charges may apply
Lock Down Publications
P.O. Box 944
Stockbridge, GA 30281-9998
Phone: 470 303-9761

Submission Guideline

Submit the first three chapters of your completed manuscript to ldpsubmissions@gmail.com, subject line: Your book's title. The manuscript must be in a .doc file and sent as an attachment. Document should be in Times New Roman, double spaced and in size 12 font. Also, provide your synopsis and full contact information. If sending multiple submissions, they must each be in a separate email.

Have a story but no way to send it electronically? You can still submit to LDP/Ca$h Presents. Send in the first three chapters, written or typed, of your completed manuscript to:

LDP: Submissions Dept
Po Box 944
Stockbridge, Ga 30281

DO NOT send original manuscript. Must be a duplicate.

Provide your synopsis and a cover letter containing your full contact information.

Thanks for considering LDP and Ca$h Presents.

NEW RELEASES

SOSA GANG 2 by ROMELL TUKES
KINGZ OF THE GAME 7 by PLAYA RAY
SKI MASK MONEY 2 by RENTA
BORN IN THE GRAVE 3 by SELF MADE TAY
LOYALTY IS EVERYTHING 3 by MOLOTTI

Coming Soon from Lock Down Publications/Ca$h Presents

BLOOD OF A BOSS **VI**
SHADOWS OF THE GAME II
TRAP BASTARD II
By Askari
LOYAL TO THE GAME **IV**
By T.J. & Jelissa
TRUE SAVAGE **VIII**
MIDNIGHT CARTEL IV
DOPE BOY MAGIC IV
CITY OF KINGZ III
NIGHTMARE ON SILENT AVE II
THE PLUG OF LIL MEXICO II
CLASSIC CITY II
By Chris Green
BLAST FOR ME **III**
A SAVAGE DOPEBOY III
CUTTHROAT MAFIA III
DUFFLE BAG CARTEL VII
HEARTLESS GOON VI
By Ghost
A HUSTLER'S DECEIT III
KILL ZONE II
BAE BELONGS TO ME III
TIL DEATH II
By Aryanna
KING OF THE TRAP III
By T.J. Edwards
GORILLAZ IN THE BAY V
3X KRAZY III
STRAIGHT BEAST MODE III
De'Kari

KINGPIN KILLAZ IV
STREET KINGS III
PAID IN BLOOD III
CARTEL KILLAZ IV
DOPE GODS III
Hood Rich
SINS OF A HUSTLA II
ASAD
YAYO V
Bred In The Game 2
S. Allen
THE STREETS WILL TALK II
By Yolanda Moore
SON OF A DOPE FIEND III
HEAVEN GOT A GHETTO III
SKI MASK MONEY III
By Renta
LOYALTY AIN'T PROMISED III
By Keith Williams
I'M NOTHING WITHOUT HIS LOVE II
SINS OF A THUG II
TO THE THUG I LOVED BEFORE II
IN A HUSTLER I TRUST II
By Monet Dragun
QUIET MONEY IV
EXTENDED CLIP III
THUG LIFE IV
By Trai'Quan
THE STREETS MADE ME IV
By Larry D. Wright
IF YOU CROSS ME ONCE III
ANGEL V
By Anthony Fields
THE STREETS WILL NEVER CLOSE IV

By K'ajji
HARD AND RUTHLESS III
KILLA KOUNTY IV
By Khufu
MONEY GAME III
By Smoove Dolla
JACK BOYS VS DOPE BOYS IV
A GANGSTA'S QUR'AN V
COKE GIRLZ II
COKE BOYS II
LIFE OF A SAVAGE V
CHI'RAQ GANGSTAS V
SOSA GANG III
BRONX SAVAGES II
BODYMORE KINGPINS II
By Romell Tukes
MURDA WAS THE CASE III
Elijah R. Freeman
AN UNFORESEEN LOVE IV
BABY, I'M WINTERTIME COLD III
By Meesha

QUEEN OF THE ZOO III
By Black Migo
CONFESSIONS OF A JACKBOY III
By Nicholas Lock
KING KILLA II
By Vincent "Vitto" Holloway
BETRAYAL OF A THUG III
By Fre$h
THE MURDER QUEENS III
By Michael Gallon
THE BIRTH OF A GANGSTER III
By Delmont Player
TREAL LOVE II
By Le'Monica Jackson

FOR THE LOVE OF BLOOD III
By Jamel Mitchell
RAN OFF ON DA PLUG II
By Paper Boi Rari
HOOD CONSIGLIERE III
By Keese
PRETTY GIRLS DO NASTY THINGS II
By Nicole Goosby
PROTÉGÉ OF A LEGEND III
LOVE IN THE TRENCHES II
By Corey Robinson
IT'S JUST ME AND YOU II
By Ah'Million
FOREVER GANGSTA III
By Adrian Dulan
GORILLAZ IN THE TRENCHES II
By SayNoMore
THE COCAINE PRINCESS VIII
By King Rio
CRIME BOSS II
Playa Ray
LOYALTY IS EVERYTHING III
Molotti
HERE TODAY GONE TOMORROW II
By Fly Rock
REAL G'S MOVE IN SILENCE II
By Von Diesel
GRIMEY WAYS IV
By Ray Vinci

Available Now

RESTRAINING ORDER **I & II**
By CA$H & Coffee
LOVE KNOWS NO BOUNDARIES **I II & III**
By Coffee
RAISED AS A GOON I, II, III & IV
BRED BY THE SLUMS I, II, III
BLAST FOR ME I & II
ROTTEN TO THE CORE I II III
A BRONX TALE I, II, III
DUFFLE BAG CARTEL I II III IV V VI
HEARTLESS GOON I II III IV V
A SAVAGE DOPEBOY I II
DRUG LORDS I II III
CUTTHROAT MAFIA I II
KING OF THE TRENCHES
By Ghost
LAY IT DOWN **I & II**
LAST OF A DYING BREED I II
BLOOD STAINS OF A SHOTTA I & II III
By Jamaica
LOYAL TO THE GAME I II III
LIFE OF SIN I, II III
By TJ & Jelissa
BLOODY COMMAS I & II
SKI MASK CARTEL I II & III
KING OF NEW YORK I II,III IV V
RISE TO POWER I II III
COKE KINGS I II III IV V
BORN HEARTLESS I II III IV
KING OF THE TRAP I II
By T.J. Edwards
IF LOVING HIM IS WRONG…I & II
LOVE ME EVEN WHEN IT HURTS I II III

By Jelissa
WHEN THE STREETS CLAP BACK I & II III
THE HEART OF A SAVAGE I II III IV
MONEY MAFIA I II
LOYAL TO THE SOIL I II III
By Jibril Williams
A DISTINGUISHED THUG STOLE MY HEART I II
& III
LOVE SHOULDN'T HURT I II III IV
RENEGADE BOYS I II III IV
PAID IN KARMA I II III
SAVAGE STORMS I II III
AN UNFORESEEN LOVE I II III
BABY, I'M WINTERTIME COLD I II
By Meesha
A GANGSTER'S CODE I &, II III
A GANGSTER'S SYN I II III
THE SAVAGE LIFE I II III
CHAINED TO THE STREETS I II III
BLOOD ON THE MONEY I II III
A GANGSTA'S PAIN I II III
By J-Blunt
PUSH IT TO THE LIMIT
By Bre' Hayes
BLOOD OF A BOSS I, II, III, IV, V
SHADOWS OF THE GAME
TRAP BASTARD
By Askari
THE STREETS BLEED MURDER **I, II & III**
THE HEART OF A GANGSTA I II& III
By Jerry Jackson
CUM FOR ME I II III IV V VI VII VIII
An LDP Erotica Collaboration
BRIDE OF A HUSTLA **I II & II**

THE FETTI GIRLS **I, II& III**
CORRUPTED BY A GANGSTA I, II III, IV
BLINDED BY HIS LOVE
THE PRICE YOU PAY FOR LOVE I, II ,III
DOPE GIRL MAGIC I II III
By Destiny Skai
WHEN A GOOD GIRL GOES BAD
By Adrienne
THE COST OF LOYALTY I II III
By Kweli
A GANGSTER'S REVENGE **I II III & IV**
THE BOSS MAN'S DAUGHTERS I II III IV V
A SAVAGE LOVE **I & II**
BAE BELONGS TO ME I II
A HUSTLER'S DECEIT I, II, III
WHAT BAD BITCHES DO I, II, III
SOUL OF A MONSTER I II III
KILL ZONE
A DOPE BOY'S QUEEN I II III
TIL DEATH
By Aryanna
A KINGPIN'S AMBITON
A KINGPIN'S AMBITION **II**
I MURDER FOR THE DOUGH
By Ambitious
TRUE SAVAGE I II III IV V VI VII
DOPE BOY MAGIC I, II, III
MIDNIGHT CARTEL I II III
CITY OF KINGZ I II
NIGHTMARE ON SILENT AVE
THE PLUG OF LIL MEXICO II
CLASSIC CITY
By Chris Green
A DOPEBOY'S PRAYER
By Eddie "Wolf" Lee
THE KING CARTEL **I, II & III**

By Frank Gresham
THESE NIGGAS AIN'T LOYAL **I, II & III**
By Nikki Tee
GANGSTA SHYT **I II &III**
By CATO
THE ULTIMATE BETRAYAL
By Phoenix
Boss'n Up i , ii & IIi
By Royal Nicole
I LOVE YOU TO DEATH
By Destiny J
I RIDE FOR MY HITTA
I STILL RIDE FOR MY HITTA
By Misty Holt
LOVE & CHASIN' PAPER
By Qay Crockett
TO DIE IN VAIN
SINS OF A HUSTLA
By ASAD
BROOKLYN HUSTLAZ
By Boogsy Morina
BROOKLYN ON LOCK I & II
By Sonovia
GANGSTA CITY
By Teddy Duke
A DRUG KING AND HIS DIAMOND I & II III
A DOPEMAN'S RICHES
HER MAN, MINE'S TOO I, II
CASH MONEY HO'S
THE WIFEY I USED TO BE I II
PRETTY GIRLS DO NASTY THINGS
By Nicole Goosby
TRAPHOUSE KING **I II & III**
KINGPIN KILLAZ I II III

STREET KINGS I II
PAID IN BLOOD **I II**
CARTEL KILLAZ I II III
DOPE GODS I II
By Hood Rich
LIPSTICK KILLAH **I, II, III**
CRIME OF PASSION I II & III
FRIEND OR FOE I II III
By Mimi
STEADY MOBBN' **I, II, III**
THE STREETS STAINED MY SOUL I II III
By Marcellus Allen
WHO SHOT YA **I, II, III**
SON OF A DOPE FIEND I II
HEAVEN GOT A GHETTO I II
SKI MASK MONEY I II
Renta
GORILLAZ IN THE BAY **I II III IV**
TEARS OF A GANGSTA I II
3X KRAZY I II
STRAIGHT BEAST MODE I II
DE'KARI
TRIGGADALE I II III
MURDAROBER WAS THE CASE I II
Elijah R. Freeman
GOD BLESS THE TRAPPERS I, II, III
THESE SCANDALOUS STREETS I, II, III
FEAR MY GANGSTA I, II, III IV, V
THESE STREETS DON'T LOVE NOBODY I, II
BURY ME A G I, II, III, IV, V
A GANGSTA'S EMPIRE I, II, III, IV
THE DOPEMAN'S BODYGAURD I II
THE REALEST KILLAZ I II III
THE LAST OF THE OGS I II III
Tranay Adams
THE STREETS ARE CALLING

Duquie Wilson
MARRIED TO A BOSS I II III
By Destiny Skai & Chris Green
KINGZ OF THE GAME I II III IV V VI VII
CRIME BOSS
Playa Ray
SLAUGHTER GANG I II III
RUTHLESS HEART I II III
By Willie Slaughter
FUK SHYT
By Blakk Diamond
DON'T F#CK WITH MY HEART I II
By Linnea
ADDICTED TO THE DRAMA I II III
IN THE ARM OF HIS BOSS II
By Jamila
YAYO I II III IV
A SHOOTER'S AMBITION I II
BRED IN THE GAME
By S. Allen
TRAP GOD I II III
RICH $AVAGE I II III
MONEY IN THE GRAVE I II III
By Martell Troublesome Bolden
FOREVER GANGSTA I II
 GLOCKS ON SATIN SHEETS I II
By Adrian Dulan
TOE TAGZ I II III IV
LEVELS TO THIS SHYT I II
IT'S JUST ME AND YOU
By Ah'Million
KINGPIN DREAMS I II III
RAN OFF ON DA PLUG
By Paper Boi Rari

CONFESSIONS OF A GANGSTA I II III IV
CONFESSIONS OF A JACKBOY I II
By Nicholas Lock
I'M NOTHING WITHOUT HIS LOVE
SINS OF A THUG
TO THE THUG I LOVED BEFORE
A GANGSTA SAVED XMAS
IN A HUSTLER I TRUST
By Monet Dragun
CAUGHT UP IN THE LIFE I II III
THE STREETS NEVER LET GO I II III
By Robert Baptiste
NEW TO THE GAME I II III
MONEY, MURDER & MEMORIES I II III
By Malik D. Rice
LIFE OF A SAVAGE I II III IV
A GANGSTA'S QUR'AN I II III IV
MURDA SEASON I II III
GANGLAND CARTEL I II III
CHI'RAQ GANGSTAS I II III IV
KILLERS ON ELM STREET I II III
JACK BOYZ N DA BRONX I II III
A DOPEBOY'S DREAM I II III
JACK BOYS VS DOPE BOYS I II III
COKE GIRLZ
COKE BOYS
SOSA GANG I II
BRONX SAVAGES
BODYMORE KINGPINS
By Romell Tukes
LOYALTY AIN'T PROMISED I II
By Keith Williams
QUIET MONEY I II III
THUG LIFE I II III
EXTENDED CLIP I II
A GANGSTA'S PARADISE

By Trai'Quan
THE STREETS MADE ME I II III
By Larry D. Wright
THE ULTIMATE SACRIFICE I, II, III, IV, V, VI
KHADIFI
IF YOU CROSS ME ONCE I II
ANGEL I II III IV
IN THE BLINK OF AN EYE
By Anthony Fields
THE LIFE OF A HOOD STAR
By Ca$h & Rashia Wilson
THE STREETS WILL NEVER CLOSE I II III
By K'ajji
CREAM I II III
THE STREETS WILL TALK
By Yolanda Moore
NIGHTMARES OF A HUSTLA I II III
By King Dream
CONCRETE KILLA I II III
VICIOUS LOYALTY I II III
By Kingpen
HARD AND RUTHLESS I II
MOB TOWN 251
THE BILLIONAIRE BENTLEYS I II III
REAL G'S MOVE IN SILENCE
By Von Diesel
GHOST MOB
Stilloan Robinson
MOB TIES I II III IV V VI
SOUL OF A HUSTLER, HEART OF A KILLER I II
GORILLAZ IN THE TRENCHES
By SayNoMore
BODYMORE MURDERLAND I II III
THE BIRTH OF A GANGSTER I II

By Delmont Player
FOR THE LOVE OF A BOSS
By C. D. Blue
MOBBED UP I II III IV
THE BRICK MAN I II III IV V
THE COCAINE PRINCESS I II III IV V VI VII
By King Rio
KILLA KOUNTY I II III IV
By Khufu
MONEY GAME I II
By Smoove Dolla
A GANGSTA'S KARMA I II III
By FLAME
KING OF THE TRENCHES I II III
by GHOST & TRANAY ADAMS
QUEEN OF THE ZOO I II
By Black Migo
GRIMEY WAYS I II III
By Ray Vinci
XMAS WITH AN ATL SHOOTER
By Ca$h & Destiny Skai
KING KILLA
By Vincent "Vitto" Holloway
BETRAYAL OF A THUG I II
By Fre$h
THE MURDER QUEENS I II
By Michael Gallon
TREAL LOVE
By Le'Monica Jackson
FOR THE LOVE OF BLOOD I II
By Jamel Mitchell
HOOD CONSIGLIERE I II
By Keese
PROTÉGÉ OF A LEGEND I II
LOVE IN THE TRENCHES
By Corey Robinson

BORN IN THE GRAVE I II III
By Self Made Tay
MOAN IN MY MOUTH
By XTASY
TORN BETWEEN A GANGSTER AND A GENTLE-
MAN
By J-BLUNT & Miss Kim
LOYALTY IS EVERYTHING I II
Molotti
HERE TODAY GONE TOMORROW
By Fly Rock
PILLOW PRINCESS
By S. Hawkins

BOOKS BY LDP'S CEO, CA$H

TRUST IN NO MAN
TRUST IN NO MAN 2
TRUST IN NO MAN 3
BONDED BY BLOOD
SHORTY GOT A THUG
THUGS CRY
THUGS CRY 2
THUGS CRY 3
TRUST NO BITCH
TRUST NO BITCH 2
TRUST NO BITCH 3
TIL MY CASKET DROPS
RESTRAINING ORDER
RESTRAINING ORDER 2
IN LOVE WITH A CONVICT
LIFE OF A HOOD STAR
XMAS WITH AN ATL SHOOTER

Printed in the USA
CPSIA information can be obtained
at www.ICGtesting.com
LVHW050245031123
762902LV00004B/343

9 781960 993304